"This is a very small town, and there are a lot of behaviors that are frowned upon..."

Brooke glanced at Jason, a provocative smile on her provocative mouth. He wanted to taste that provocative mouth.

"Are we having the sex talk?" she asked.

"It's not a sex talk," he protested, then rubbed his face where his scar was starting to throb. "It's more of an anti-sex talk. I know you think you're attracted to me, but hell, Brooke. I don't want a woman in my bed because I bought her a shirt."

It was the wrong thing to say...because off came her shirt. Jason tried desperately not to stare at the twin mounds of taut flesh. He failed.

"It's your shirt. You think I want to sleep with you because you gave me a shirt? Okay, then. No shirt. No problem."

He felt his mouth grow dry; his groin started to ache. "Put on the shirt."

She smiled, ran a hand through her hair, dark against her perfect ivory skin.... "No."

"Please," he asked nicely, hearing the crack in his voice.

"No, I'm an adult, capable of following my instincts. And if your shirt is going to get in the way..."

Jason darted his gaze av didn't help.

He was doomed.

Blaze

Dear Reader,

I come from a very frugal family. As a kid, I never realized this because we had the world's greatest toys. A mismatched swing set, a yellow rickshaw, and this great brass bell that you had to hand-crank to bong (and yes, it did not ring, it *bonged)*. I still own a chair made out of a tractor seat, and in our den sits a lamp made out of an old water pump.

Eventually, it dawned on me that it was not little elves that were making these toys for us, but my dad. After I was married, the husband and I bought ten acres of land in the Texas Hill Country. And I saw the same enterprising tendencies there.

In Texas, there are a lot of hands-on folks who know how to fix a car, how to saw down a tree, and can do all their own electrical work without missing a beat. I love that pioneer spirit in the Lone Star State, and I took full advantage of it when creating Jason Kincaid.

It's always hard to say goodbye to all the characters in a series, and this one was no exception. I hope you have loved the Harts of Texas as much as I do.

Best,

Kathleen O'Reilly

Kathleen O'Reilly

JUST GIVE IN...

™ Harlequin®

TORONTO NEW YORK LONDON
AMSTERDAM PARIS SYDNEY HAMBURG
STOCKHOLM ATHENS TOKYO MILAN MADRID
PRAGUE WARSAW BUDAPEST AUCKLAND

Recycling programs
for this product may
not exist in your area.

ISBN-13: 978-0-373-79639-7

JUST GIVE IN...

ABOUT THE AUTHOR

Kathleen O'Reilly wrote her first romance at the age of eleven, which to her undying embarrassment was read aloud to her class. After taking more than twenty years to recover from the profound distress, she is now proud to finally announce her career—romance author. Now she is an award-winning author of nearly twenty romances published in countries all over the world. Kathleen lives in New York with her husband and their two children who outwit her daily.

Books by Kathleen O'Reilly

To get the inside scoop on Harlequin Blaze and its talented writers, be sure to check out blazeauthors.com.

Don't miss any of our special offers. Write to us at the following address for information on our newest releases.

Harlequin Reader Service
U.S.: 3010 Walden Ave., P.O. Box 1325, Buffalo, NY 14269
Canadian: P.O. Box 609, Fort Erie, Ont. L2A 5X3

To the big-hearted people from the big-hearted state.
Texas, forever.

_1_

EVERY FAMILY STARTED with a house, a mother, a father and a passel of squabbling siblings. Brooke Hart had no father, two unsociable brothers who seemed deathly afraid of her and a 1987 Chevy Impala.

As far as families went, it wasn't much, but it was a thousand times better than before. Then there was the mysterious message from an estate lawyer in Tin Cup. They needed to "talk" was all that he said, and apparently lawyers in Texas didn't believe in answering machines and voicemail, because every time she tried to call, no one answered. In her head she had created all sorts of exciting possibilities, and journeyed cross country to see the lawyer, bond with her brothers and find a place to call home, all of which was exciting and expensive, which meant that right now, she was in desperate need of a job. Money was not as necessary as say, love, home and a fat, fluffy cat, but there were times when money was required. One, when you needed to eat, and two, when your three-year-old Shearling boots weren't cutting it anymore.

In New York, the boots had been cute and ordinary and seventy-five percent off at a thrift store. In the smoldering

September heat of Texas, she looked like a freak. An au courant freak, but a freak nonetheless.

As she peered into the grocery store window, she studied an older couple who were the stuff of her dreams. In Brooke Hart's completely sentimental opinion, the spry old codger behind the cash register could have been Every Grandpa Man. A woman shuffled back and forth between the front counter and the storeroom in back. Her cottony-gray hair was rolled up in a bun, just like in the movies. The cash register was a relic with clunky keys that Brooke's hands itched to touch. The wooden floor of the grocery was neat, but not neat enough, which was the prime reason she was currently here.

They looked warm, hospitable and in desperate need of young, able-bodied assistance.

The one advantage to living with Brooke's mother, Charlene Hart, was that Brooke knew the three things to absolutely never do when searching for a job.

One. Do not show up drunk, or even a more socially acceptable tipsy. Future employers frowned on blowing .2 in a Breathalyzer.

Two. Do not show up late for an appointment. As Brooke had no appointment, this wasn't a problem.

And the last, but most important rule in job-hunting was to actually show up. Although Brooke believed that deep down her mother was a beautiful spirit with a generous nature and a joyous laugh, Charlene Hart was about as present in life as she was in death, which was to say, not a lot.

Frankly, being family-less sucked, which was why she had been so excited to track down her two brothers. Twenty-six years ago, a then-pregnant Charlene Hart had walked out on Frank Hart and their two young sons, Tyler and Austen. Seven months later, Brooke had been born in a homeless shelter in Oak Brook, Illinois. Charlene never spoke of Frank, or her sons. Charlene had rarely spoken of anything grounded in reality, and it wasn't until after she died that Brooke found an article about Tyler Hart on the internet. After feeling so alone for all her life, she had stared at the picture of her brother, with the same faraway look in his dark eyes, and the world felt a little less gray. She knew then. Over and over she had repeated her brother's name, and Brooke realized she wasn't family-less after all.

To better appeal to her brothers, she'd concocted the perfect life. Storybook mother, devoted stepfather, idyllic suburban residence, and a rented fiancée (two hundred bucks an hour, not cheap). But her brothers had clearly never read the Handbook on Quality Family Reunions, and although they'd been polite enough, their shields were up the entire time. If they found out the truth of Brooke's less than storybook existence? A disaster of cataclysmic proportions. Relatives never reacted well when poor relations with no place to call home showed up on their doorstep. They weren't inclined to "like you" or "respect you" or even "want to be around you." Oh, certainly, they might act polite and sympathetic, but homelessness was a definite black mark, so right now, she wasn't going to let them find out.

And then, when the time was right, Brooke would spring the truth on the boys, and work her way into her new family's good graces.

Her first step involved getting a job, paying her way, shouldering her own financial burdens. Second, find out what the lawyer wanted.

Slowly she sucked in a breath, bunching her sweater to hide the green patch beneath the right elbow. In New York, the mismatched patch looked artsy, chic-chic, but to two elderly citizens, it might seem—frivolous. Finally satisfied that she looked respectable, Brooke walked through the rickety screen door, catching it before it slammed shut.

The friendly old proprietor gave her a small-town-America smile, and Brooke responded in kind.

"I'm here about the job. I think I'm your girl. I'm energetic, motivated. I have an excellent memory, and my math skills are off the charts."

The man's jovial mouth dwindled. "We didn't advertise for help."

"Maybe not, but when opportunity knocks, I say, open the door and use a doorstop so that it can't close behind you."

Behind her, she heard the door creak open, as if the very fates were on her side. Her spirits rose because she knew that this small grocery story in Tin Cup, Texas, was fate. Emboldened, Brooke pressed on. "When I saw this adorable place, I knew it was my perfect opportunity. Why don't you give me a try?"

The old man yelled to the back: "Gladys! Did you advertise for help? I told you not to do that. I can handle the store." Then he turned his attention to Brooke. "She thinks I can't do a gall-darned thing anymore."

From behind her, an arm reached around, plunking a can of peas on the wooden counter. The proprietor glanced at the peas, avoided Brooke's eyes, and she knew the door of opportunity was slamming on her posterior. She could feel it.

Hastily she placed her own competent hand on the counter. "My brothers will vouch for me. Austen and Tyler. I'm one of the Harts," she announced. It was a line she had clung to like a good luck charm.

At the man's confused look, she chuckled at her own misstep, hoping he wouldn't notice the shakiness in her voice. "Dr. Tyler Hart and Austen Hart. They were raised here. I believe Austen is now a very respectable member of the community. Tyler is a world-famous surgeon."

She liked knowing her oldest brother was in the medical profession. Everybody loved doctors.

The man scratched at the stubble on his cheek. "Wasn't that older boy locked up for cooking meth?"

Patiently Brooke shook her head. If the man messed up this often, she would be a boon to his establishment. "No, you must have him confused with someone else."

A discreet cough sounded from behind her, and once again the proprietor yelled to the back. "Gladys! Which one of the Hart boys ended up at the State Pen?"

Astounding. The man seemed intent on sullying her family's good reputation. Brooke rushed to correct him, but then Gladys appeared with four cartons of eggs stacked in her arms. "There's no need to yell, Henry. I'm not deaf," she said, and then gave Brooke a neighborly smile. "He thinks I'm ready to be put out to pasture." She noticed the can of peas. "This yours?"

"It's mine," interrupted the customer behind her.

Not wanting to seem pushy, Brooke smiled apologetically. Gladys placed the eggs on the counter and then peered at Brooke over silver spectacles. "What are you here for?"

"The job," Brooke announced.

"We don't need any help," Gladys replied, patting Brooke on the cheek like any grandmother would. Her hands were wrinkled, yet still soft and smelled of vanilla. "Are you looking for work?" she asked. Soft hands, soft heart.

Recognizing this was her chance, Brooke licked dry lips and then broke into her speech. "I'm Brooke Hart. I'm new in town. I don't want to be an imposition on my family. Not a free-loader. Not me. Everybody needs to carry their own weight, and by the way, I can carry a good bit of weight." She patted her own capable biceps. "Whatever you need. Flour. Produce. Milk. And I'm very careful on eggs. People never seem to respect the more fragile merchandise, don't you think?"

Gladys looked her over, the warm eyes cooling. "You look a little thin. You should be eating better."

The hand behind her shoved the peas forward, sliding the eggs close to the edge. Smartly, Brooke moved the carton out of harms way.

"I plan to eat better. It's priority number two on my list—right after I find a job. I'm really excited to be here in Tin Cup, and I want to fit in. I want to help out. Perhaps we could try something on a temporary basis." She flashed her best "I'm your girl" smile. "You won't regret it."

"You're one of the Harts?" asked the old man, still seeming confused.

"Didn't think there was a girl. Old Frank hated girls." From the look on Gladys's face, Gladys was no fan of Frank Hart, either.

"I never actually met my father," Brooke explained, not wanting people to believe she was cut from the same rapscallion cloth. "My mother and I moved when I was in utero."

"Smartest thing she ever did, leaving the rest of them," said Henry.

Brooke blinked, not exactly following all this, but she needed a job, and she sensed that Mr. Green Peas was getting impatient. "I really need a job. My brother Austen will vouch for me."

Gladys's gray brows rose to an astounding height. "Nothing but trouble, that one. Stole from Zeke..." Then she sighed. "He's doing good things now, with the railroad and all, but I don't know."

"That was a long time ago." Henry chimed in, apparently more forgiving.

"It's getting even longer," complained the man behind her.

Gladys shook her kindly head. "We're not looking to hire anybody, and you being a stranger and all. No references, except for your brother…"

"I'm new in town," Brooke repeated in a small voice, feeling the door of opportunity about to hit her in both her posterior and her face, as well. Doors of opportunity could sometimes be painful.

"I'll vouch for her."

At first, Brooke was sure she had misheard. It had happened before. But no, not this time. Brooke turned, profoundly grateful that the goodness of small-town America was not overrated. She'd lived in Atlantic City, Detroit, Chicago, Indianapolis and six freezing weeks in St. Paul. She'd dreamed of a little town with bakeries and cobblestone streets and hand-painted signs and people who smiled at you when you walked past. She'd prayed for a little town, and finally she was about to live in one. "Thank you," she told the man behind her.

He was tall, in his mid-thirties, with chestnut brown hair badly in need of a cut. There wasn't a lot of small-town goodness emanating from the rigid lines of his face. A black patch covered his left eye and he had a thin scar along his left cheek. In fact, he looked anything but friendly, but Brooke didn't believe in judging a book by its cover, so her smile was genuine and warm.

"You know her, Captain?" Gladys asked.

Mr. Green Peas nodded curtly. "It seems like forever."

"It's about time you're making some friends in town. We

were worried when you moved out to the old farmstead, not knowing a soul in town and all. I'll tell Sonya, she'll be happy to hear that."

Not sure who Sonya was, but sensing that Captain's opinion counted with these two, Brooke faced the couple. "Please, give me a job," she urged. "You won't regret it."

From somewhere in the tiny grocery, Brooke could hear a relentless pounding. A rapid-fire thump that seemed oddly out of place in the sleepy locale.

Thumpa-thumpa-thumpa.

Gladys and Henry didn't hear the loud noise.

No one did.

Because, duh, it was her own heart.

She told herself it didn't matter if she didn't land this job with this homespun couple. It didn't matter if her brothers didn't welcome her with open arms. It didn't matter if the lawyer had made a mistake.

She told herself that none of it mattered.

All her life Brooke had told herself that none of it mattered, but it always did.

Her hands grasped the counter, locking on the small tin can. "What do you say?"

Gladys patted her cheek for a second time. Soft, warm... and sorrowful.

"I'm sorry, honey. We just can't."

As rejections went, it was very pleasant, but Brooke's heart still crawled somewhere below the floor. They had been so friendly, the store was so cute with its handpainted Hinkle's Grocery sign over the door. She'd been so sure. Realizing that there was nothing left for her in this place, Brooke walked out the door, opportunity slamming her in the butt.

Her first day in Tin Cup. No job, no lawyer, an uneasy brother who didn't know she was here, and—she glanced down at the can of peas still stuck in her hand—she'd just shoplifted a can of peas. Brooke fished in her jeans pocket for some cash, brought out two crumbled dollars, an old Metro Card and a lint-covered peppermint—slightly used.

Two dollars. It was her last two dollars, until she found a job, of course. All she had to do was go back inside, slap the money on the counter and leave as if she didn't care. As if they hadn't shouted down her best "Pick me!" plea.

Brooke turned away from the store with its cute homespun sign and restashed her money. Better to be branded a thief than a reject. It wasn't the most honorable decision, but Brooke had more pride than many would expect from a homeless woman that lived out of her car.

Once she was gainfully employed, she'd pay back Gladys and Henry. They'd understand.

And was that really, truly how she wanted to kick off her new life in her new home? As some light-fingered Lulu, which apparently all the Harts were supposed to be, anyway?

After taking another peek through the window, she sighed. No, she wasn't going to be a light-fingered Lulu, no matter how tempting it might be. And especially not for a can of peas.

In the distance a freckle-faced little girl on a skateboard careened down the sidewalk. Eagerly, Brooke waved her down, hoping to recruit an unwitting accomplice so that Brooke Hart wouldn't be another unflattering mug shot on the Post Office wall.

"Hello," she said, when the little girl skidded to a stop and then Brooke held out her hand. "Can you give this to Gladys? Tell her it's for the peas."

The girl examined the proffered money, then Brooke, innocent eyes alight with purpose. "You going to tip me for the delivery?"

Yes, the entrepreneurial spirit was strong in this one. Who knew that honesty was such a huge pain in the butt? And expensive, too. After jamming her hand in her pocket, Brooke pulled out her last seventeen cents. Reluctantly, she handed it to the kid, who stood there, apparently expecting more.

"Please?" asked Brooke, still wearing her non-stranger-danger smile. At last, the little girl sighed.

"Whatever," she said and kicked a foot at the end of the skateboard, flipping it up into her hand.

"That's pretty cool," Brooke told her, and the girl rolled her eyes, but her mouth curled up a bit and Brooke knew that she'd made her first friend in Tin Cup. Sure, she'd had to pay for the privilege, but still, a friend was a friend, no matter how pricey, no matter how small.

"Whatever," the girl repeated, then pulled open the screen door.

Now that Brooke's fledging reputation was somewhat restored, or about to be, her job here was done. She dashed across the street, leaping into her eyesore of a car before anyone could see. She had big plans before she showed up on Austen's doorstep, and it wasn't going to be without a job, without any money and in a car that should be condemned.

Once safely behind the wheel, she tossed the can of peas onto the backseat, the afternoon sun winking happily on the metal. It fit right in with the hodge-podge of things. A portable cooler, one beat-up gym bag, her collection of real estate magazines, the plastic water jug and now peas.

Peas.

What the heck was she supposed to do with peas?

2

THE LED WAS blinking a steady green over his front porch, the motion detector nearly hidden beneath the old wood doorframe. From inside, he could hear the sound of a dog barking.

All clear.

Not that anyone was going to break into his less than fancy house, but old habits were hard to break. There was no dog, only a pimped out robotic vacuum cleaner with two golden LEDs for eyes and a mechanical tail that wagged. Not the cutest puppy, but Jason Kincaid had invented the only canine in the world that cleaned up after itself.

While Dog wheeled around the floor, Jason put down his keys, pulled on his faded Orioles cap and went outside to work. The missing can of peas didn't concern him. Jason hated peas, but every Monday he went to the Hinkle's store to shop. He hated shopping, too, but his father had told him he needed to get out more, so every Tuesday when his dad called, he could tell the old man—with complete honesty—that he'd been out shopping only yesterday.

Outside the house, the flat terrain was exactly the same. The front yard, the backyard, the four storage sheds and even the detached one car garage were filled with lawn mowers, vacuum cleaners, small engines, large engines, lumber and scrap metal.

He'd never invited his family to visit because the house looked too much like a junkyard, like the long neglected habitat of a man who needed to live alone.

Which it was.

Jason pulled down the socket wrench from the upright mattress springs that had been recycled into his Wall O' Tools and got to work.

The current project was a five horsepower lawnmower in desperate need of a new carburetor or a humane burial, but Jason wasn't ready to give it up for dead. Not yet.

He'd just gotten air to blow clean through the tube when the red LED on the porch began to glow. Motion detectors had been strategically placed across the ten acres of his land, wired to let him know whenever anyone decided to intrude—like now. Jason glanced toward the road and noticed the cloud of dust.

A HAV, or, in layman's terms, a car still unidentified.

Salesmen didn't come out this far. He'd never met the neighbors, which were four acres away on either side, so when people showed up at his gate, they were usually lost.

After pulling his cap down a little lower, Jason made his way to the front gate, an eight foot, black, metal monster that he'd rescued from an old sanitarium. It looked exactly like it belonged at the front entrance of a sanitarium, which was why Jason had wanted it, and why the sanitarium didn't.

From behind the iron bars, he watched the beaten-up Impala approach. The rear door was black, the driver's side door was red, and the hood was sunshine-yellow. If Henry Ford and Picasso had gone out on a bender, that car was what the hangover would have looked like.

Jason stayed steady and impassive, not angry or

unfriendly, but stood and watched as a woman exited the world's worst excuse for a car.

Her.

She still had the same never-say-die smile, which, considering the state of her transport, was just flat-out stupid. Once she was at the gate, a mere two feet from him, she held up the can of peas.

"You left these." Her voice was nice, not high and bird-like, but no cigarette smoke, either. Sonya had a low, husky voice. At one point, Jason had thought it was sexy.

"You didn't have to bring them all the way out here." He probably should thank her for it, but he was distracted by the beads of sweat on her neck, and the green sweater had to be hot. Judging from the way it was clinging to her curves, the Hell-Car didn't have air-conditioning. He didn't like that she was sweating for him. He didn't like the way his one good eye kept locking on her chest, like some reconnaissance tracking system doped up on Viagra.

"I don't mind," she told him, then put the can to the bars, as if she expected the can to slip through. Nope. Jason could have told her that metal didn't work that way. It took five hundred pounds of force to dislodge metal, or eight hundred degrees of heat. Sometimes both.

However, Jason stayed silent because he had learned that people never liked to work too hard at a conversation. Eventually, they always gave up.

"Are you going to open the gate, or should I toss this sucker over the top?"

His instinctive response was to instruct her to go ahead and throw, but two things kept him from going with the default. The knowledge that he would have crossed the crazy-lonely-man line in his head, and the beat-up sedan. Frankly, that car out-crazied his crazy-line anyway, so while she might not notice, he would.

Those were his reasons. That, and he liked her breasts.

He typed in the combination on the keypad and the gate creaked open. He'd gone through a lot of trouble to get the creak exactly right. A haunted house creak. At the sound, the woman's eyes grew wide, but not in fear. *No, she liked it.*

"I bet the kids love this place at Halloween."

"People don't drive out this far for a stick of gum." People didn't drive out this far for peas, either, but he left that part out.

"If they don't, they don't know what they're missing." While she talked, her eyes surveyed the yard, the seventy-year-old house, the mountains of scrap, the piles of engines.

Before she could trespass farther, he took the can of peas. "Thank you." Then he nodded once, held the gate open and politely waited for her to leave.

Leaving didn't seem to be part of her strategy. She ducked under his arm and wandered inside, looking at one pile, then the next. "What do you do with this stuff?"

Jason shrugged, not about to explain his hobbies to her, and not sure he could. Not that anyone would understand, anyway. Hell, he didn't even know why.

His gaze followed her as she walked around, moving from one mound to the next, drawing precariously close to the house.

His pulse rate kicked up. Anxiety or lust? She was cute, short, stacked and curious. The clothes were out of place in the September heat, but he was grateful she was covered up, cause he didn't think his pulse rate could handle any more. He liked her hair though. It was long, dark silk that hung down her back.

"What is that?" she asked, pointing to a modified bicycle. "Wait, wait, don't tell me."

Not that he would have told her anyway, so he stayed

quiet while her fingers traced over the twisted metal hump with the leather seat mounted on top. Crouching down, she inspected the spring-loaded frame with the four iron-spoke wheels. It'd taken him three months to find the wheels, and eventually he'd bought them on eBay. They were perfect.

"It's an animal?"

Still he waited.

She rose, studied the thing. "First, there are four legs, or wheels. Second, the elongated back is almost like a hill… or a hump…" Her finger crept to her mouth, chewing absently. She had a nice mouth. Red lips that spent most of their time open. His mind, always running in a tangential yet somewhat practical direction, began to think of all the uses for an open mouth: eating, breathing, kissing, sucking.

Her mouth opened wider. "A camel!"

And now that twenty questions were over, Jason needed to send her on her way. As he headed to the metal gate, he thanked her for coming. There was very little sincerity in the words, but he didn't think she would notice.

Her dark eyes flickered once. Okay, she noticed. He kicked a particularly heavy cast-iron drum. The pain was solid, well deserved. His foot would recover.

"That's some car."

Back and forth she shifted, like she was embarrassed about her mode of transport, but after seeing his mode of habitat, he couldn't understand why she would care.

"I bought it in Tennessee."

"Long drive for a car," he noted, realizing he was making conversation, lingering in her company.

It was her breasts. Had to be.

Evil breasts.

His body hardened at the thought of touching her evil breasts.

"Tennessee was on the way," she responded, hopefully not tuned in to his thoughts.

"Surprised the car made it," he told her, channeling his thoughts into another more socially-acceptable direction.

Seeing her wince, he made a mental note to stop commenting on the dicey condition of her vehicle, but it was a little hard to ignore. The inside of the car appeared to be in as bad shape as the outside, with a blanket thrown over the backseat like a tarp. The tarp was most likely designed to keep out prying eyes—like his own. A gallon jug of water was sitting in the front seat, some food wrappers, a pillow, a half-open gym bag and a small sack for trash.

Her home.

As he continued to stare at her mode of habitat, a flush crept up her face, and he knew her habitat was a taboo conversation topic, too. That worked out well for him since he wanted her off his place.

All of her, including her breasts.

"You're staying with your brother?" he asked pleasantly. As parting remarks went, it wasn't the best.

"Oh, yeah," she answered quickly, moving to stand in front of her car, blocking his view.

"Good," he said, not that he believed her. Considering the state of her car, her finances, he didn't think she was related to anybody in town. If she had family, she would have gone there first.

Probably the brother thing was a lie, as well. In which case, she'd be jobless, living out of her car...

Not that he cared.

She reached for the door handle and yanked it open, the damn thing sticking so hard that her shoulder was now probably dislocated.

Jobless, dislocated shoulder, living out of her car...

Not that he cared.

"You need a job?" he asked, sounding exactly like he was offering her a job. The woman turned, her eyes swimming with hope—until it was gone.

"You know someone who's hiring?" she asked, her eyes not so hopeful, unless a man was looking.

"I need some help here," he offered, thinking quickly. "Organizing."

Not that he wanted organization, not that he wanted human companionship, especially of the female variety, especially of the homeless, jobless female variety.

Most likely, she was needy.

His old army buddies would be laughing their asses off.

Of course, if any of them saw her breasts, they would understand.

"I'm a great organizer," she said, hands clasped tight in front of her, prayer-like, and he realized how much she wanted this.

A job.

Not him.

Not that he was even thinking sex. A man who lived in a junkyard with one good eye was no prize. Nope, Sonya had made that clear, and that was long before his junkyard phase.

No, it wasn't the sex. It was the idea of this woman being out there alone. Jason might not be the biggest people-person in the world, but sometime people deserved better. Sometimes—rarely, but sometimes—Jason noticed.

"It'd be temporary," he added, in case she thought he was charitable.

"That'd be perfect. It'll give me a chance to settle in town and find a permanent position."

"Yeah. I can't afford a lot," he said, in case she thought he was loaded.

"I don't need a lot," she told him, obviously guessing he wasn't loaded.

"Good." They stood there and stared for a minute, and she didn't seem to mind his eye patch. Since she was going to be working for him, not shrinking in horror was a plus.

Finally she spoke. "I'm Brooke Hart."

"Jason Kincaid." He should have offered her his hand, but he didn't. A handshake implied a contract, a pledge. This was nothing more than one human being helping out a woman who needed a chance to get her life together.

Not that he cared.

"So, you're staying with your brother?" he asked again, in case she wanted to come clean about her living situation.

"Yeah," she answered, not coming clean. *Message received. Don't ask about the living situation, either.*

"You can start tomorrow?"

"First thing."

"Not too early. I don't get up early," he lied. Jason got up at the crack of dawn, but he thought he should straighten up his place first. Get things in order before she started... organizing.

"Not a problem. I have a lot of things to do." She paused. "With my brother."

"Sure," he agreed like an idiot. Rather than letting her notice that he actually was an idiot, he headed back toward the gate.

"I'll see you tomorrow around ten. That'll be okay?"

The smile was back in place.

Not that he cared.

Then she nodded and climbed into the Hell-Car. Once he returned to the yard, he spent the rest of the day repairing an old wheelchair. Yet every time he looked toward the porch, it was the red LED that was lit, not the green. Sometimes animals set off a false positive, but not often, and not tonight. Someone was out there, or maybe some-one had never left.

When night fell, and the crickets began to chrip, Jason quit working and then walked along the fence line, a man with no particular purpose at all. When he was a kid, he had sat on the porch with his dad, watching the sky and the stars, talking baseball and trusting the world to pass by peacefully.

After thirteen years in the army, he knew better. As he walked the fence line, he spotted what he'd been searching for. The old Impala, parked at the edge of the fence line. One dim reading light glowing from the interior.

It was dark outside and she was still out there.

Obviously no brother. No place to stay, but at least she now had a job. A temporary job.

Not that he cared.

There were a lot of things to do before tomorrow. Make the house habitable for human living, do some laundry and throw out the two-month old milk in the fridge. And while he was doing that, she would be out there alone. He tried to ignore the hole in his gut. There was nothing that he could do about the Impala that was parked at the edge of the road, but every few hours, he peeked out the window, making sure there was no trouble.

Not that he cared.

BROOKE CALCULATED THAT by day three she would have enough money to buy more suitable work clothes. First, she needed a cooler shirt, because the sweater was a merino-wool blend that was causing her to wilt. In order to have money for the car, she had sold most of her clothes in Nash-ville. At that time, a sweater had seemed practical. Now, not so much. The Shearling boots were looking sadder by the minute and would need to be replaced, too. Brooke believed that no matter the financial hardship, it was important to look capable and confident.

Unfortunately, the work that the Captain had given her was insultingly easy, as if she wasn't capable of anything more. That morning, he'd handed her a sheet of paper and then indicated a knee-high pile of assorted mechanical whatsits, a tiny island in a yard of complete chaos.

"Here. Write down everything you see."

"That's an inventory, not an organizational system," she pointed out, and he glared at her out of his one visible eye, which he probably thought was intimidating, but she thought it was more sexy pirate. She knew he wouldn't want to hear that, so she pulled her features into some semblance of lemming-hood.

He didn't look fooled. "Inventorying this pile is step one. Once that's done, we'll talk about step two."

She nudged at a wheelless unicycle with her boot. "It's going to take me fifteen minutes to do this. Why don't you let me sort by type?" By all indications, he'd tried to do that in the areas closest to the house. Wood boards were stacked together, some kind of electric gizmos were lined up like bowling pins—wait, they were bowling pins.

He put his hands on his hips, doing that intimidating thing again. "You don't know what each item is."

Unintimidated, she picked up a springy thing attached to a weight with a circular metal plate on the end, some piece of the Industrial Revolution that'd gotten left behind. Probably on purpose. "You really know what this is?" she asked.

At the Captain's silence, she dangled the part higher in the air.

As a rule, Brooke was usually a people-pleaser, but she had issues with someone thinking that poor people didn't have a brain in their head. It was apparent that the Captain was giving her busy-work in order to give her money because he felt sorry for her. Charlene Hart would have taken the money and ran, possibly stopping for happy hour on the way. Brooke Hart needed people to see her as something more than a charity case—someone positive, someone good.

His gaze raked over her, inventorying her clothes, but lingering on the thingamaboobs beneath. Wisely Brooke pretended not to notice. "You're not dressed for working outside," he told her, because apparently his optimal working wardrobe was a thousand-year-old pair of jeans, a white undershirt, and a denim work shirt that hung loose on his rangy shoulders. Perhaps if Brooke had discretionary funds, she might have sprung for something more functionally appropriate. But no, she decided, even if she were as rich as Trump, she still wouldn't be caught dead in clothes that were so...démodé.

Not wanting to argue about her outfit, she held the doodad up higher, just so that he would notice her chest. Cheap, yes, but effective. "You don't know what this is, do you? Insulting my clothes won't detract me from the truth. Exhibit one, an antiquated widget that got rusted over in the Ice Age."

He muttered under his breath. "I'll give you money. Go into town. Buy something. At least better shoes."

And now she was back to being a charity case. Brooke placed the doo-dad on the ground and pushed up her sleeves. "I'm here to work."

"You can't work in those shoes."

Seeing the stubborn set to his jaw, Brooke decided that there was no point in continuing the discussion. She walked toward the front gate, skirting one hill then another. A demonstration to the unbelieving that her boots were just fine.

Unattractive? Yes, but this was from a man who thought exterior appearances unimportant. Or at least she hoped so.

"Where are you going?" he yelled, just as she reached the gate.

"I can't work under these conditions. You're trying to micro-manage everything and I'm accustomed to more responsibility. I suggest you find some able-bodied teenager who needs detailed instruction and doesn't mind a dress code."

"It isn't a dress code," he yelled back. "More a dress suggestion."

She turned, stared him down in silence until finally he shrugged.

"You win. I won't say another word about your clothes."

Still, there was disagreement in his face. Brooke stayed where she was. "I can help you with your inventory, but you have to let me do my job. Do you have a computer I can work on?"

"In the house."

"Good. I can use the computer to look up whatever I don't know, and you can work in peace. We'll get along fine, and I'll guarantee you'll be happy with the results."

At his nod of agreement, she picked a path from one pile to another, until she stood in front of him. Once again, his gaze drifted to her boots.

Brooke held up a hand in warning. "If you can't say anything nice, don't say anything at all."

Judging by his four-letter response, it was a rule he needed to work on, but Brooke was down with that.

Like she'd said, if he'd let her do her job, they'd get along fine.

BY THE TIME THE SUN was baking overhead, Brooke had sorted and inventoried fourteen small heaps of contraptions that no man in his right mind would want, which only proved her suspicions that the Captain was a standard left-brainer. As even more evidence, not that she needed it, inside the house was a veritable smorgasbord of oddly designed gizmos and wuzzits. A push-button car radio hooked up to an iPod. Bookshelves made from stacked wooden pallets, a vintage Coke machine made into a bar and a small metal box with a blinking light that made her nervous.

That, and then there was Dog. The little, rounded 'pet' scooted around the floor at different speeds, and sometimes he sang "Happy Birthday, Mr. President," in a voice that sounded just like Marilyn Monroe. Some dog, indeed.

Everything seemed to belong in an art gallery, a museum or thrift store, possibly all three, but she had to give him high marks for creativity. Brooke would've never thought of an automated pot scrubber or a self-cleaning toilet. However, now that she'd seen them, she wondered why no one had ever thought of them before.

Judging from the never-ending materials she had left to inventory, he'd be making gizmos for the next two hundred years. A long trickle of sweat dripped in her eyes, and she dreamed of moving to the coolness of the house, but there were only three more piles to sort, and then she'd be done. Better to go forth and succeed, then celebrate an honest day's work. Hopefully, air-conditioning would be involved.

Out of the corner of her eye, she could see the Captain watching her from the other side of the yard. In order to demonstrate her non-wimpiness, she hefted a ten-inch fly-wheel motor (thank you, Google) and placed it in a neat line with the others, before noting the type on her list. It was only after she had deposited the oily thing that she knew why he was staring. In the middle of the sweater was a su-persized grease stain that no amount of artistic cover-up could disguise. Sensing the beginnings of another lecture, she waved happily, but it was too late.

The Captain advanced.

"I owe you a new sweater. That one's ruined." There was a glint in his eye as if he'd been waiting for just this moment.

Nuh-uh-uh.

Pulling at the wool, Brooke shot him her sweetest smile. "It looks like a map of Canada. I think it's just the touch it needed."

His jaw twitched.

"At least put on a cooler shirt."

Certainly there was a logic to that. He seemed to be genuinely concerned, and she considered the idea, but it was only Day One, Hour Six. He'd given her a nonsense job, and now he wanted to put her in his clothes like some vagrant. So what made her different from any other hard-luck case on the mean streets of life?

Absolutely nothing, and Brooke Hart wasn't just some other hard-luck case. No, she was going to work this off with grit and sweat, and probably a lot more grease, and the Captain would just have to deal.

Of course, she'd already put in a lot of grit and sweat. Fourteen piles were now neatly inventoried and identified. Maybe a cooler shirt was a fair trade, an old-fashioned barter sort of arrangement. Yeah, that seemed reasonable, and she was just opening her mouth to accept his offer, when he lifted a can of some unknown substance and threw it on her sweater.

Brooke's mouth snapped shut as the wool plastered to her stomach like a skin mask gone bad.

Aha.

The unknown substance was glue.

3

As THE SUBSTANCE BEGAN to dry, Brooke glared at the Captain, trying to find some words. Although as a rule she wasn't usually a believer in violence and/or retribution, she felt here there were extenuating circumstances. Her hands fisted into small glue-encrusted WMDs.

Before she could move (flexibility was difficult when epoxified), he set the can at her feet, pushing a hand through his dark hair.

"I don't think I should touch you but...ah, hell, Brooke, I'm sorry, but we need to get you cleaned up." Oh, sure, now he looked sorry.

She plucked the sweater loose from her stomach, wincing as if she were in pain, just so he'd feel worse. "What's the plan now?" she asked. "Hose me down with turpentine?"

He paused, trying to decide if that was a joke. Comprehension dawned slowly, and his mouth twitched with humor. "I wouldn't have used a hose. Go shower before you harden and turn into yard art."

Not a big fan of his sense of humor, Brooke stalked inside. If there had been a carpet or a rug, she would've worried about dripping. Not that she had any business being worried, since this was all his doing, but still…a nice rug would have done wonders for the faded wood floors, and given the place a marvelous homey appearance.

She found the bathroom, painted in a surprisingly cheery buttercup-yellow. His quiet footfall sounded behind her—so stealthy for such a big guy.

"I imagine this will take some time. The towels are where?" she asked, happy to see his face still covered in guilt.

The Captain held up a pair of large scissors.

Brooke frowned. "That isn't a towel."

"Unless you want glue in your hair, you'll need to cut the sweater, and, uh, anything else I screwed up."

Cut? *Cut?* Was he out of his mind? Didn't he know this was high-quality apparel? "I'm not cutting this."

"It's gone. Let it go. I'll replace it." His smile didn't look so sad, and that was when she knew, when his win-at-all-costs behavior became apparent.

"You did this just so that I'd have to trash it."

He nodded. "Reason and logic weren't winning the war. Sometimes covert maneuvers work best."

And still he didn't see the problem. "Aren't you the least bit sorry?"

"Of course," he said, sounding sincere…mostly.

Her eyes narrowed. "But you'd do it again, wouldn't you?"

At her words, he wanted to lie. She could see the denial building on his face, but no, the man was damned to tell the truth.

"Probably. Although I'd have come up with something a little less drastic than accelerator glue. The smell's killer. I didn't get any in your hair, or your face?" He frowned. "Are you allergic to anything?"

"A little late to ask." She grabbed the scissors, shut the door, and got to work destroying her most favorite sweater.

After two not-so-awesome tries, she could see this was going to be a problem. The wool was hard, getting harder by the second, and the glue was mucking up the scissors. Determined to avoid asking for help, she hacked on, but the scissors were getting worse, and her fingers were starting to stick, and from outside the door, she could hear him pacing.

Three more times she tried, three times she failed, and finally, Brooke sighed. The shabby girl in the mirror wasn't responsible, or plucky, or capable of surviving whatever life threw at her. Dark hair stuck out in sweat-damp clumps. Her wonderful sweater was now crusted over with a glossy sheen that looked wrong.

Her brothers would disown her...again. Maybe she didn't have much, but she had her pride, she had her self-respect and she had a body that was uncomfortably stiff. All because of him. No, the Captain was going to pay for this and pay big. Slowly she smiled, the girl in the mirror looking less shabby by the minute. Thoughts of revenge did that to a woman.

Flinging open the door, Brooke brandished the scissors like a sword. "Ruined. Do you have something better? A blowtorch maybe?"

He studied her partial sweater-ectomy. Then he scratched his jaw, where the darkened stubble was starting to show. "Nah. Glue's flammable."

"This is no time for sarcasm."

"Not sarcasm. Look it up."

She glared. He shrugged. "Give me a minute."

Less than thirty seconds later, he was back with a hunting knife capable of great destruction. The Captain's face was tense, waiting for her to take the knife, but that wasn't part of her plan, and so she spun around, giving him her back. "Make a clean cut, neck to hem," she instructed. "You didn't get any glue back there. It should go easier."

The air crackled with his fear. "You're sure about this?"

"Just do it," she whispered in a teasing, taunting voice.

Gently he pulled aside her hair and in one quick slice, the sweater hung in two loose pieces, her back bare except for the single bra strap.

"You can...uh...handle the rest?" His words were rough, hesitant...awkward.

Oh, yes, revenge was a dish best served hot.

Brooke whirled around, plucked at the sweater's remains and then pulled it off, standing before him in jeans and bra. His eye flickered, mouth tightening, but to his credit, he didn't look down. Not once. The man had the self-control of a monk.

Well, pooh. However, Brooke wasn't done. Not by a long shot.

With a sticky-fingered snap she unhooked the front fastening, tugging at the tacky material, finally ridding herself of the bra, which was a genuine la Perla and had set her back an even fifty bucks.

Still the man didn't look.

Here she was, stiff and uncomfortable, flaunting herself like some cheap tart. The least he could do was pay attention. Drastic measures were called for.

"You know, I might need mineral spirits for these babies, after all. Got some?"

This time, the eye flickered and his face flushed, the scar turning a liquid silver. One gray eye met hers, the same hot liquid-silver color as his scar. Brooke's skin bloomed hot, then cold, the remains of the glue clinging to her chest, making her damp, moist, sticky...

Nope, not just the glue.

She thought he was going to touch her, was dying for

him to touch her, but instead he spun on his heel and walked away.

"One can of mineral spirits, coming right up."

4

JASON FLEW TO THE BACK shed before she spotted the tiny drop of glue on her knee and decided the jeans had to go, too.

God.

The word was a curse and a prayer, a testament to what a woman's bare breasts could do to a man's good intentions.

The shelves in front of him were filled with paint and oil and transmission fluid, and as his eyes scanned the contents, he realized that he didn't have any damn mineral spirits.

Not that she needed mineral spirits on those beauties. The dusky hue of her nipples needed nothing more than a touch, a taste. No, chemicals would be a crime against nature. His fingers flexed, itched, copping a cheap feel from a nearby paint can that did absolutely nothing to relieve his pain.

Now what the heck was he supposed to? Her little striptease was payback, teasing, a cock-busting joke for throwing glue on her.

And *who* had thought of the glue?

No, he was going to have to face her, pretend that he'd never seen her naked, pretend that all this was no big deal.

After pulling down a tin of degreaser, he glanced at the no-big-deal bulge at his fly. She wouldn't miss that. No, she'd laugh at his misery. She'd think that he deserved it.

Which he did, but he didn't want her to know that.

Only one way to take care of that problem. Efficiently, Jason unzipped his jeans, taking matters into his own hand, and five minutes later, he was back to his normal-size piston, and all it had taken was the mental image of Brooke Hart, naked with dark-fire eyes, open-mouthed invitation, taut, perky breasts and the arousing shimmer of epoxy.

Oh, he'd been alone too long.

Once again, he felt the pull in his balls, the hardening in his cock, and he groaned in sexual agony.

Another ten minutes. That'd do it.

He was sure.

Maybe.

THEY BUMPED ALONG the road in the Captain's pick-up, a tense ride because apparently the man wasn't up to having a conversation.

Maybe she'd gone too far, maybe she'd ruined the image that she'd been going for. Slutty, instead of spunky. But slutty was preferable to pity.

She peeked at his profile, the right side of his face so normal, so capable. Then she thought of his bad eye, his scar. Lots of people would pity him, and he would hate it, just like she did.

It was a short drive to the heart of Tin Cup. Her new hometown. Her first day in Tin Cup, she'd tried to find the law offices of Harris and Howell, but only located lawyer Hiram Hadley. After hammering on his door for ten minutes, the dry cleaner next door said that he was in North Dakota taking care of his father who'd been ill. Other than that, she'd had little desire to explore, since she wasn't eager to find Austen until she'd got herself in a more suitable situation. Still, she was deathly curious about this place, so she scanned the picturesque landscape, the neat clapboard homes, the rangy mesquite trees. It was so different from the places she'd been before, but the sight of the planters lining Main Street cheered her. It felt like home.

Not that she wanted to meet anyone when she was dressed like this. The Captain had given her a large, drab olive T-shirt. Though neatly tucked into her jeans, the shirt still looked wrong. That, and she wasn't comfortable being without a bra. She crossed her arms over her chest, and he glanced at her. Then down.

Brooke smiled tightly.

"I shouldn't have ruined your sweater." This time, he sounded appropriately chastened. A no-holds-barred flash-job could do that to a man.

"No, you shouldn't have."

"Aren't you going to apologize, too?" he asked, apparently believing that she shared some blame in ruining her sweater.

"No," she told him in a cheery, blame-free voice.

The Captain blew out a breath. "You don't know me. You shouldn't take stupid risks with someone you don't know."

This time, she blew out a breath. "Life is all about risks, taking chances. It doesn't matter how safe and comfortable you want things to be. They never are."

"No," he agreed. "I'm sorry."

This time he wasn't apologizing for the sweater. He was apologizing for all the hardships in her life, which didn't make her any happier. "I don't want to be your cause du jour."

"I don't believe in causes."

She doubted that, but kept quiet.

"You don't have to sleep in your car," the Captain said, braking at the lone stoplight in town.

"Inviting me to sleep somewhere else?" she teased. She wanted to hear him say it. She wanted to hear him admit that he wanted her. Some of it was pride and ego, some of it was that she wanted to be wanted, but the most urgent part was that she wanted him.

Charlene Hart wasn't a fan of upstanding men. She liked her men footloose and flawed. And in the ten years since her death, Brooke hadn't moved in the sort of circles where soft-hearted men roamed.

The soft-hearted man next to her looked at her, one eye that clearly saw so much. "No invitations. You can take the couch."

She shrugged, as if it didn't matter.

Moments later he turned down Main Street, pulling to a stop in front of a tidy row of shops. The Hinkles' grocery was there, a post office, Dot's Diner and Tallyrand's. "It's not Paris, but Tallyrand's has some good shirts. And shoes."

Then he passed her a credit card. "Get what you need."

She stared at him, squared her shoulders. "I'll pay you back."

"I know."

Then she smiled, liking his confidence in her, liking the way the sun played in his hair. The Captain needed a haircut, and tomorrow, she would tell him. "Thank you."

"Your brother should take you in." He paused. "If he is your brother."

Did he have to ruin it now? "You don't ask me questions, I won't ask you any, either."

The Captain nodded. "Fair enough. Get what you need. An hour's enough time?"

"More than enough."

TWO HOURS LATER, and Brooke had yet to show up at the truck. Jason considered leaving her in town, but as tempting as the idea was, it was a hot afternoon, and he couldn't bring himself to abandon her.

Her or her breasts.

Deciding that he had to find out, he made his way through the seven stores of downtown Tin Cup before finally tracking her down in the same place she'd started—Tallyrand's. Tallyrand's was a combination feed and clothing store, owned by Rita Tallyrand, who was the former Ms. Pecos Valley back in 1957. It wasn't the sort of personal detail that Jason usually remembered except that Rita reminded everybody each time they came into the store.

"Captain!" Rita called out, and Jason managed a smile, immediately spotting Brooke next to the shelves full of shirts. She was still wearing his old T-shirt. Two hours of shopping and zilch to show for it?

Jason closed his eyes, telling himself to be patient, but then Rita waylaid him and he knew escape was impossible. What was worse than a nightmare?

"Captain," she whispered, eyes fixed on Brooke. "You know her? Gladys said you knew her. Who is she? One of the Harts? There was no girl, but that's how she introduced herself. Said she was a sister. I wanted to call the Sheriff, to find out what's what, but the Sheriff was out babysitting for Mindy. Have you seen the new baby?"

It was gossip like that that kept Jason far away. "No."

Rita frowned. "No, you don't know her?"

"I know her," he volunteered, choosing not to divulge any more of the pertinent facts he knew about her, not that they were facts, exactly. More supposition, he supposed.

"She's a Hart?" Rita asked again.

Now this was where it got tricky. Jason knew that Gillian

Wanamaker and Austen Hart were tight, and if he told Rita that Brooke was a Hart, and it turned out that Brooke wasn't a Hart, but part of some wild, best-forgotten weekend from Austen Hart's past, then Gillian would be crashing down Jason's door because not only did Gillian Wanamaker have a possessive streak, but she was the sheriff, and also carried a gun.

After glancing at Brooke, he laughed in a knowing way. "She's not a Hart. Not even a family friend. Seems like she read about the Hart family troubles and thought the whole thing was romantic in a Bonnie and Clyde trailer trash sort of way. Too much television in her life," he added, not wanting Rita to think that Brooke was mentally unstable or anything.

Rita still eyed Brooke suspiciously. "She's been browsing in the shirt section for two hours. Maybe Gladys is right about the girl's possible sticky fingers, although I don't see where she could hide a shirt."

"She's a good kid."

Rita shot him a curious look. "Not a kid."

Rather than confirm that Jason knew she wasn't a kid, but a healthy, well-developed woman, he chose to keep his mouth shut.

"Can you get her out of here?" Rita asked. "I want to close up and make it home before I miss the news."

There was nothing more that Jason would like than to get her out of here. As he approached her, Brooke smiled and motioned him closer.

"I can't decide between the darker blue with long sleeves, or this plain cotton tee. The long-sleeved one is better quality, but—" she glanced at Rita and pitched her voice low "—it's a little pricy."

Patiently Jason removed both shirts from her hands and gave them to Rita. "We'll get them both."

Brooke grabbed the shirts back. "No. We won't. One shirt."

Rita watched the exchange, not saying a word. Smart lady.

However, Jason knew that Brooke wasn't going to give in. Part of him understood her need to make it on her own. Part of him thought she was an idiot for being too stubborn, and part of him, a very masochistic part, wanted to see her naked again.

"One shirt," Jason agreed. That was his hard-on talking.

"Which one?" Brooke asked, holding up one shirt then the other.

"The blue one looks nice with your hair," Rita offered, now realizing that money would eventually change hands.

Brooke flipped over the price tag, chewed on her lip. "But it's so expensive."

"All cotton," Rita explained. "And look at the seams. You're not going to get that sort of stitching for a song."

And still Brooke shook her head. "I don't know."

Slowly Jason counted to ten.

"It's worth every penny."

Brooke chewed on her lip. "I don't know. Maybe if it was...oh, ten percent less. Then I wouldn't feel so extravagant."

Jason counted to twenty this time. Didn't help.

Rita considered the offer and finally nodded.

"Ten percent, but only because you're a friend of the Captain's."

"My family is from here," Brooke said, following Rita to the register. Rita turned, giving Jason a knowing wink.

"Well, sure, sweetie. Is this cash, check or charge? I'll need four forms of ID if you're writing a check."

Brooke handed her Jason's credit card. "Charge, please. I'll need the receipt."

Jason knew the instant that Rita read his name on the card.

"Credit is so fast these days," Rita murmured, folding up the shirt. "Just one quick slide and then, whoops, look what you've done."

"I don't believe in credit myself," Brooke told her, noting the frilly bookmarks displayed on the counter, studying each one carefully. "It's too easy to lose your head."

Rita looked at Jason. "Isn't it, though?"

This time Jason counted to ninety-nine in multiples of three. Still didn't help.

After Rita handed the bag to Brooke, she smiled. "You'll be staying with the Captain?"

"Oh, no," Brooke laughed, as if the idea was ludicrous. "He's my boss."

Rita raised her brows. "Really?"

Brooke laughed again, not so quickly this time. "I needed a job, and he offered me a position at his house. Inventory. I think I'd like to organize things a bit better. It's a little chaotic." She pulled the package tight to her chest. "I'm new here. I'm trying to start off right. I know I'm a stranger, but I hope you'll give me a chance."

Seeing the sincerity in Brooke's face, Rita thawed. Jason understood. "We don't get much entertainment out here, so sometimes we make up our own."

Brooke leaned in closer. "I know exactly what you mean. Maybe sometime I could come in and chat?"

Through the window, Jason could see the setting sun and he wanted nothing more than for this day to be through. "I think Rita wants to close up," he told Brooke, in case she decided that now was a good time to chat.

Rita clucked her tongue. "They are *always* impatient, aren't they?"

Brooke laughed and Jason hurried her out the door.

ON THE DRIVE BACK, Jason watched as Brooke took out her new shirt and laid it over her lap. Her fingers worked the buttons, and he realized that this was a woman who wasn't used to a lot of clothes.

"I'm sorry about the sweater," he apologized again, but this time, he felt like words weren't enough.

"I wouldn't have kept it," she told him with a forgiving smile, as if it didn't matter, but Jason knew she would have kept that sweater until she died. The right thing to do would be to buy her a new sweater. Something pretty. Something nice. Something extravagant.

"I'm sorry about what Rita was thinking," he continued. Apparently, today was the day that apologies were flowing like wine. Sonya had always hated that he never apologized.

"She thought we were having sex. It's not a big deal." Brooke's head was down, dark hair hiding her face from view.

"It wouldn't be if it were true, but it's not, so it is a big deal." He sounded like the world's biggest prude, but he didn't mind. He didn't know why he didn't mind, but when Brooke smiled up at him, he knew he'd said the right thing.

"I can cook dinner for you if you like."

Such nice words, such dangerous words. In the back of his head, Jason knew this wasn't smart, but on the other hand, he didn't want her to starve, either.

"I have a frozen pizza, not much else." It wasn't meant to be an invitation. But it was.

"A frozen pizza and a can of peas," she reminded him with a smile that shot straight to places he'd rather not be thinking about right this second, but like a dog, he kept on thinking, anyway. He kept on panting, too, kept on remembering the sight of her perfect breasts.

A tiny voice urged him to take, but there was something in her eyes that held him back. He saw desire there, sure, but also he saw gratitude, and he felt as if he should lay out the ground rules before she did something they would both regret.

"Brooke?"

"Yes?"

Suddenly, a rabbit jumped across the road, and Jason swerved to avoid it. Brooke fell against him, her hand clutching his thigh, his engorged crotch.

Damn.

Quickly, her hand was gone, and Brooke shot to the opposite side of the bench seat. It was safer with her there.

Jason cleared his throat. "This is a very small town, and there are a lot of behaviors that are frowned upon."

She glanced at him, a provocative smile on her provocative mouth. He wanted to taste that provocative mouth.

"Are we having the sex talk?" she asked.

"It's not a sex talk," he protested, then rubbed his face where his scar was starting to throb. "It's more of an anti-sex talk. This is a dangerous situation and I know you think you're attracted to me but, hell, Brooke. I don't want a woman in my bed because I bought her a shirt."

It was the wrong thing to say because off came her shirt. Jason tried desperately not to stare at the twin mounds of taut flesh. Failed. "Can we please wear our clothes?"

She turned, offering her breasts before him like some buffet plate. "It's your shirt and you think I want to sleep with you because you gave me a shirt. Ergo, no shirt. No problem."

His mouth grew dry, his cock started to ache and his

foot was pushing as hard as it could on the gas. "Put on the shirt."

She grinned and ran a hand through her hair, dark against her perfect ivory skin. "No."

"Please," he asked nicely, hearing the crack in his voice.

"No. I'm an adult, capable of following the call of my loins, and if your shirt is going to get in the way..."

Jason kept his eyes on the road, but it didn't help distract him from his desire for her. Up ahead he could see his long, gravel drive. His bed, her laying across his bed, wearing nothing but him.

"Brooke," he tried again, not looking. Damn. He was looking. The woman had the most perfect set of breasts on the planet, and apparently she wasn't shy about showing them off.

This was probably how Hart got in trouble with her. They were probably somewhere in Vegas, she pulled off her shirt and kapow. Circuits were fried, good intentions were lost and sex was had. Halfway up the drive, he slammed on the brakes because he needed clothes on her before they made it to the house. In the truck, there were rules, gearshifts. In the house, all bets were off.

"Is there a problem?" she asked, laying her arm across the back of the seat, so hot, so warm, so...

"Brooke," he repeated, pleading, since all he wanted to do was touch her, kiss her, take her. Her fingers tiptoed across the edge of his seat, flicking against his neck. It was the first time she'd ever touched him.

Jason turned, met her eyes firmly. "No."

She cocked her head. "You don't want me?" She knew he did, but he couldn't tell her. It was the last armament keeping him in check.

"I don't want you."

Her hand slid from his face to his hard-on. Softly, tortuously, she squeezed. "Liar."

"This isn't right."

Brooke slid closer, her breasts brushing against his arm, and he could smell his soap on her, his shampoo. "Kiss me. Make it right."

As she said the words, she licked her lips and that was all he could take.

Jason grabbed her, pulled her astride him, and devoured her mouth like the starving man he was. Her fingers stroked his hair, his face. So long, too long. He explored her mouth with his tongue, feeling her warm welcome. It was like drowning.

His hands grabbed her breasts, knowing exactly where to touch, and she arched into him, riding his cock like they were already there.

He wanted her already there. He wanted inside her. He wanted to feel her. All of her. With clumsy fingers he attacked her fly, feeling the metal give, sliding beneath the rough denim, finding…her.

His finger thrust inside her, and she nipped at his lip, and Jason knew he wouldn't make it to the house.

It had been so long. She felt so good. His finger pushed harder, higher, feeling the wet heat. Each time he thrust, she rode him. Hard, sure…sweet.

A woman at a vulnerable place, a woman who needed respect and patience.

Sweetness.

Some of his calm returned and he kissed her again, trying to take things gentle and slow. Her mouth tasted like peppermint and fire and her hips kept arching toward him, riding him…loving him.

Patience?

He was going to die.

"Take me here, Captain. Please."

Her hands poised over his fly, waiting.

And who was he to stay no? Resigned to his fate, Jason opened his one good eye, stared at his house, blinked twice, and then prayed that his vision was wrong.

Survival instincts kicked in, he pushed Brooke aside and fumbled for the damned shirt.

"What's wrong?" asked the topless woman who didn't think that modesty was a good thing.

Wrong? She had no idea of the trouble her breasts were about to get them into. Everything was wrong because approaching the truck in her ridiculous heels was Sonya.

Seeing the other woman, Brooke finally had the sense to cover herself. "Who's that?" she asked, and he could hear the hurt in her voice. He hated the hurt.

"I'm Sonya Kincaid. Mrs. Sonya Kincaid."

Brooke gasped, but before she could kill him Jason clarified the situation. "Ex. She's my ex."

5

OUT OF THE THREE OF THEM, Brooke was the only one completely relaxed. Inside the house, Sonya was perched on a barstool and the Captain brooded unhappily on his couch. Brooke pulled in a footstool from the porch and prepared to watch family dynamics in action. On television, families fought and then laughed, all in a thirty-minute interval punctuated with fast-food commercials. In shelters, families never fought, only stared ahead, silent and shuttered, not wanting to give anything away. Brooke suspected reality was somewhere in between.

She glanced curiously back and forth, until Sonya flushed pink.

"Could we have some privacy?" asked Jason's former wife in a snippy voice that Brooke thought was stress rather than a natural condition.

"I could go out to the car," Brooke offered cheerfully.

"She's a guest," the Captain said. "She stays."

At his words, Brooke looked at Sonya and shrugged innocently.

"Why don't you tell me why you're here?" the Captain asked his former wife. Sonya Kincaid was very pretty in a very blond way and was wearing a sleek red suit that matched her lipstick perfectly. She wasn't what Brooke would have expected of the Captain's ex-wife. She was way too neat, but maybe that explained the divorce.

Sonya brushed at her skirt, which was immaculate like the rest of her. "Aunt Gladys called last night. I had been planning to drive out to see you anyway, so I decided it was time to stop by. She was concerned. We all are."

The Captain scowled. "You drove out here for nothing."

Sonya nodded at Brooke. "Apparently not."

Sensing the tense undercurrents in the room, Brooke felt it was time to clarify the situation. "Primitive sexual urges are completely normal. No reason to worry about that. Giving in to our animalistic nature is inevitable."

Sonya rolled her eyes. "Oh, please. You're taking advantage of Jason, and there's no one out here to put a stop to it."

The Captain stood and glared at his former wife. "Get the hell out." His voice was low, gruff, and it was the first time that Brooke felt a shiver of fear.

Quickly, Sonya gathered her purse and started for the door, but Brooke called out before she could leave.

"Wait. Don't go like this. You walked in on an awkward situation. I'm sure that seeing your ex locked in a torrid embrace with someone new was difficult, and you've got a right to be a little bitchy." Brooke winked at the Captain. "But we're all mature adults here, and I know the Captain is a big enough man to forgive you." Then she smiled at him. "Isn't that right?"

Sonya didn't seem happy, but at least her nostrils had lost that pinched look. She stared at the Captain, and Brooke waited, hoping that she'd done the right thing.

Finally the Captain waved a hand, and Sonya sat. "So why are you here?"

"Can we discuss this in private?" Sonya asked, apparently not one to learn from her mistakes.

"No. Brooke stays."

Once again, Brooke shrugged innocently and Sonya sighed. "I want to talk to you about the test well."

Test well? Now Brooke was intrigued. This was oil country, the land of black oil and undiscovered riches. *Her home.*

"No," snapped the Captain, apparently not so intrigued.

"Why?" his former wife asked, a perfectly reasonable question in Brooke's opinion.

"After the discharge, I moved out here to be by myself. The last thing I want is people hanging around here."

"You need the money," Sonya argued.

"You mean you need the money," the Captain replied. "You have the house in Killeen. I have this place. You got the better deal. Case closed."

Sonya glanced at Brooke. "Let's not have this argument in front of the girl."

Brooke grinned. "Don't mind me. I'm thinking of making popcorn."

"Jason!"

"Brooke," the Captain warned.

Brooke held up her hands to keep the peace. "No popcorn."

By now the Captain's color had returned to normal, his scar faded to the color of bone, and Brooke was happy to see the smile at the corners of his mouth. He was having a good time...just like she'd intended.

He leaned back against the couch, legs splayed, the faded jeans clinging to powerful thighs that were as hard as bricks. Remembering exactly how they felt beneath her, Brooke felt a momentary throb between her legs, a reminder of an itch that had yet to be scratched. Secretly, she checked the digital clock on the wall. Eight-seventeen. It was still early. Darn it.

"How's Tom?" the Captain asked.

Sonya crossed her legs, uncrossed her legs. "He left, and please don't lecture me. I don't want to hear it."

"I'm sorry," the Captain said, and his former wife's eyes were wide with surprise.

"Did you love Tom?" Brooke asked, which was not any of her business, but Sonya seemed heartbroken and Brooke wanted to know exactly who had broken her heart. The Captain or this Tom?

"I thought I loved him." Sonya peeked under lashes at the Captain, apparently still fostering some hope. "I was wrong."

While the Captain watched his former wife, Brooke held her breath. If there were still feelings involved, she certainly would get out of the way. It was the honorable thing to do, but...

Brooke frowned, not nearly so intrigued anymore.

Sonya stood. "I'll leave now. I'm sorry for interrupting. Think about the well, Jason. At least then you could hire someone to haul away this junk."

Brooke kept quiet, this wasn't her concern, and after she heard the door close, she found the Captain watching her. There was no fire in his gaze, no feeling at all.

The apathy hurt, and she wished it didn't.

"There's a bunk in the shed outside," he started, and Brooke managed a smile.

"I'll sleep in my car. It's more comfortable and I bought this goose-feather duvet in Oklahoma. It's very nice." Brooke moved toward the door, but the Captain took her arm before she could leave.

"I'll take the shed. Sleep in the bed. You need the rest."

Okay, rest wasn't what she'd been thinking. The Captain

noticed her look, and his hand fell away. "I knew this wasn't smart."

"You still love her?" Brooke hadn't meant to ask, but the words were out before she could stop them.

"No. A long time ago I was stationed at Ft. Hood. I met Sonya. We got married. After I was in Iraq, she met Tom. Three months later we were divorced."

And instantly Brooke understood the depths of Sonya's betrayal. Wishing she could do more, Brooke covered his hand, marveled at the strength, the competence, the heart within him.

For a moment he held on before opening the door. Brooke frowned, wondering what she had missed. "Why are you leaving?"

He touched her hair, smiled sadly. Somehow the Captain seemed worldly wise. "It's not right."

"You think I'm taking advantage of you?"

"No. I think I'm taking advantage of you."

The anger simmered slowly inside her, building, spilling over into something more dangerous. "Do I look stupid?"

The Captain took a cautious step back. "No."

"Then why have you decided that this is a bad idea? You were a happy man earlier. You seemed thrilled." She glanced at his crotch. "All of you."

The Captain flushed. "It was a mistake. You're in an uncertain situation. I'm the only person you know in Texas."

"Except for Austen," she reminded him.

The Captain's expression was alarmed. "I don't think it's a good idea for you to see him."

Brooke sighed. "Well, no, not until I get back on my feet. And I will," she added, seeing his skepticism.

"I know, but sex confuses things."

She glared. "Do I look confused?"

"No."

"Are you confused?"

"No."

Somehow the Captain could be very dense. "Then why are you still wearing clothes?"

This time, she was happy to see an appropriate level of apprehension. "You haven't eaten," he pointed out, an obvious stall tactic, and Brooke took a predatory step closer.

"If I was hungry, I would say so. I have a tongue in my head. I know how to use it."

The Captain took another step back. The door snapped shut.

"This is gratitude," he argued.

Her hands went to the hem of her T-shirt.

"Not the shirt. Not again." He swore, and Brooke realized that she needed to change her tactics, so she did.

She came to him, rose up on her toes, and laid her head on his heart. It was a good heart, a noble heart, and Brooke was pleased that Sonya had thrown him over.

Sonya was an idiot.

Ever so slowly, his arms wrapped around her, iron bands made of steel. Everything faded to silence, except for the beat of her blood. He tilted her chin, met her eyes, giving her a last chance to leave. However, he felt right, this felt right, and she reached up to trace the jagged edge of his scar with a gentle touch.

Instead of letting her touch him, the Captain bent, covered her mouth with his, kissing her urgently, with no gentleness at all. His strong hands skimmed lower, molding her hips to his, and when she felt the hard ridge honing between her legs, Brooke groaned happily.

This was what she wanted, he was what she wanted. He pulled her shirt over her head, and his mouth moved to her breast, her nipple, sucking until the flesh was taut and needy. The stubble on his jaw was rough against her skin, a friction that was both pleasure and pain.

There was something about this man that spoke to her, aroused her. Underneath the scars and the machines was a man who cared. A man who didn't want to.

Tonight, she wanted to give him what he had given her. Peace. Hope. Happiness.

Needing to feel him, she tore at the buttons on his shirt, ruining a perfectly good garment, but his mouth was making her crazy, the prodding pressure between her legs was making her crazy. Her hands explored the smooth planes of his back. With her lips she tasted the warm salt of his neck, and her fingers teased his nipples until he told her to stop. The couch was too far, the floor so convenient, and they fell there, the Captain stripping off her jeans and her panties, thrusting a finger inside her. Her eyes locked with his, the gray darkened to smoke. With each stroke, her muscles pulsed, the pressure building higher and higher.

It was like nothing she'd ever felt. The pleasure, yes. The security, no, and that was the most erotic thrill of all. Her nails dug into the wall of his shoulders, anchoring there because her body was about to explode.

She could see the sheen of sweat on him, feel the strain in his body, his arms. Total control.

Her legs flexed and she shuddered, and still his hand moved. Faster, harder...

Yes...

A low whimper broke from her and when she was ready to come, he stole his finger from her. She whapped at his back, but then his mouth trailed kisses down her breasts, her stomach. With rough hands, he parted her legs, and Brooke's heart stuttered and then threatened to stop.

She couldn't survive this. It was too much.

Head bent, he sucked at the skin of her inner thigh,

playing, then tracing with his tongue. Because the Captain was an evil man, one finger traced her plump outer lips, lazy, insidious, diabolical.

Her hips arched up to meet him, to beg him, to kill him, but she could tell that he liked seeing her like this, liked her incoherent speech.

"Please," she managed, when his finger slid inside her, his mouth a whisper's breath away. Then his tongue flicked once, tempting her pulsing core, and the world started to spin.

Her fingers tangled in his hair, not teasing at all. A push, a pull, anything, anything.

This time, his tongue flicked twice.

Brooke yelped.

His hands gripped her thighs, and this time, oh, yes... this time.

His tongue moved over her, sucking her swollen lips, her clit, sucking her soul. She was going to explode, she was going to die.

The next thing she knew, she was floating, and she could hear her name. He was saying her name.

"Brooke?"

She opened heavy eyes and seeing the Captain's worry, she smiled. "Mmm?"

"You haven't had enough to eat. You passed out."

She grabbed him by the neck, pulled him down, and gave him her best "not hungry for food" kiss. The Captain, being an astute man, kissed her back, slid his cock between her thighs, and with one powerful thrust, the world went golden again.

JASON PRAYED SHE WASN'T going to faint because he needed to come. She was so hot, so wet, so perfect. Brooke was every man's fantasy, every man's dream, but the thin smile on her face was cause for concern. Each time he thought of pulling out, her muscles pulled him in, locking him there and, oh, hell…

Over and over he thrust, his balls pulling tight. Just when he knew he was going to explode, her eyes opened and stared, taking in his face, his body, and he waited for her to look away. Instead, she smiled, the world's most beautiful smile. A man could drown in the light of her eyes, and there was nothing he wanted more. Her legs tightened around him, her muscles clenched, and the smile turned to something more carnal.

"Captain," she whispered in invitation, and that was all. His muscles froze, his back arched, and he wanted to roar. But there was only one sound, one word he could say.

"Brooke."

THREE HOURS LATER, the Captain had prepared frozen pizza, topped with peas. It wasn't gourmet, but for Brooke, it hit the spot. Her other spot. Apparently tonight the Captain was two for two. They ate on an old army trunk that the Captain had rigged up for a table. As he had pulled the heavy trunk in front of her, he apologized, saying that he wasn't used to company. Considering the man was doing his heavy lifting in the nude, Brooke had added in a lot of unnecessary directions, simply because she liked to watch him move.

His body was long and lean, with muscular thighs, powerful arms and, not that she was going to tell him, but his ass was divine. Made for a woman's hands. Like hers, for instance.

His face fascinated her, too. The scar and eyepatch were an odd counterpoint to the full lips, and there was a dimple on his chin as well. Before his accident, she suspected that he'd had a very boyish appearance. Now, he looked like a man who had shouldered the world without complaint.

Brooke finished her slice and downed her beer, and then watched as Dog wheeled the dishes to the sink.

"He's very helpful," she commented, watching as the tray was shuttled from floor to sink with the help of a pair of grips attached to a robot arm.

The Captain watched the arm extend, frowning when one fork got caught in the grip. The arm pushed, contracted, pushed, contracted, and eventually the fork fell in the sink. "I don't use it a lot," he explained, and she knew that by tomorrow morning, it would be fixed.

"Why don't you patent any of this?"

Long legs stretched out in front of him, and he shook his head, his hair still tangled by her hands. "That's too much work."

She supposed that living alone, the Captain was accustomed to being nude. Since Brooke had grown up with communal bedrooms and bathrooms, had always had a roommate, privacy was a luxury that she couldn't afford, and it was never wise to be nude when living in a car. Most of her life had been spent in pajamas. Until now.

She yawned, watched his eyes lock onto her breasts and smiled.

Yes, nudity was nice.

His cock stirred and, well, she found herself fascinated by the chain of action and reaction.

The Captain noticed. "You haven't been in a lot of relationships, have you?"

"More than enough," she answered truthfully. Although she'd had sex several times, she'd never been in a relationship. Charlene Hart had set a poor example and Brooke had met too many men who didn't understand the word *no.* She had learned very quickly and very painfully that a woman with little money, traveling alone, was a target for predatory men.

"How well do you know Austen?" he asked.

"He and Tyler were in New York last year." She winced at the memory. "The meeting didn't go over as well as I'd planned, but this time, I think I have it. A more independent, less needy approach."

He reached out, touched her hair. "Take your time. Get your house in order. Did you have enough to eat? There's some frozen dinners in there, too. I could heat one up."

"No, and next time, we'll have real food. I'll cook," she offered. It was obvious that the Captain didn't.

"No need," he said and once again his gaze tracked over her, lingering and then sliding away. The Captain stood, picked up the clothes scattered about, and pulled on his jeans.

"I'll be in the shed. Use the shower. Yell if you need anything."

And yes, they were back to the sleeping arrangements. Brooke rose, artfully stretching like a cat. "A shower would be great." She pulled up her hair, rolled her neck and then winced.

Instantly he was at her side. "Are you okay?"

"I must have some kinks to work out. You have some sort of massager gizmo, do you? I would love that—" she told him, reaching around and kneading one shoulder, then the other "—right here." She thrust her chest out, a flagrant cry for attention that a woman would have recognized immediately. Then she put her palms on her rear. "And here."

The Captain looked pained. "I don't think I have anything that can help."

There was an instant when Brooke considered abandoning her quest, but she couldn't in good conscience kick him out of his bed, and besides, she wanted him to hold her again. It was for these reasons that she launched into a series of stretching positions designed solely to make him see things from her point of view.

When she flexed her arms, he licked his lip.

At her toe touches, he actually groaned.

Yet still, the man resisted.

Finally she stalked over, put his hands firmly on her ass and sighed. "These are killing me. Can you just rub a little? And put some muscle in it, if you wouldn't mind."

The Captain removed his hands, grabbed her and pulled her toward the shower. "It's easier this way. Trust me."

THE CAPTAIN HAD BUCKETS and buckets of hot water and she was glad he had no massaging gadgets, because his hands, his mouth and his cock worked best of all.

He rubbed her muscles until she wept and then he stood behind her, entered her and made her weep again.

When she was sure there would be no more arguments about where he would sleep, he dried her off, put on his jeans, grabbed a pillow and headed for the front door.

Furious and naked, Brooke raced after him, and dragged him inside. "Do not think I have used all the weapons at my disposal."

At first, she thought she'd lost, but then the Captain tapped his chin and his mouth twisted into a magical smile. "Really?"

This time he didn't argue, and she pulled him under the covers, curled up a decent one foot away from him and waited. Eventually his arms crept around her, and Brooke fell into a deep, satisfied sleep.

JASON WOKE WITH Brooke's hair in his face, her thigh on his cock, and one full breast branding his arm. No matter how much he needed to, he couldn't move. The softness of a woman's skin, the fresh smell of her hair. It'd been a long time.

Brooke sighed in her sleep and Jason frowned. He had questions about her past, her family, all the things that he didn't understand, but he knew better than to ask. Maybe the answers would scare him, maybe the questions would send her away, or maybe the questions would bind her to him tighter.

So instead he lay there, watching her sleep, her body wrapped about his like a vine. He knew her body, he'd used her body, but it was her face that he tried to avoid. Seeing with one eye didn't make him blind. She was wary, she was innocent and she trusted him completely.

It was the Stockholm syndrome with the kidnapping part. Now what was he supposed to do with her? He had yet to tell her that Austen was living with the Sheriff, and Jason had heard rumors the two would be married soon. The last thing the Sheriff would want was her soon-to-be-husband's former-weekend-fling staying with them—even if she didn't have a place to live. Nobody could be that understanding. And since Austen wasn't an option, Jason couldn't send her away. Nor could he keep her.

She stretched, her thigh rubbing him, and her lips pressed a kiss to his shoulder.

While his brain wondered what he was supposed to do with her, her fingers closed over him and began to move.

She shifted over him, giving him a full-bodied good-morning kiss that had him instantly awake. Her body rose high, she pushed back the dark curtain of her hair, and he didn't understand why this goddess was in his bed.

Not that he was complaining.

As if they had all the time in the world, she arched in the sunrise, the light skimming her breasts, and he wanted to touch her, but his hands stayed firm at his sides.

Then she smiled at him in the way that only she could, and he fisted his hands. She leaned over him, kissing his torso, his chest, continuing lower until her vulnerable mouth closed over him. Jason shut his one good eye because this way, he could be blind. For the moment at least, he was blind to everything but her.

THE NEXT DAY TURNED as hot as the one before, but while she worked out in the yard, Brooke was getting to like the feel of the sun on her skin. The West Texas landscape was so flat that it seemed to stretch forever. The trees were stubby and squat and, in the distance, she could see oil wells pumping steadily. It was only day two, but already she'd left her mark. The old milk crates she found were much more suitable than the small mountains the Captain had created. And more portable. He had argued that he needed the crates for another project.

"All fifty-three of them?" she asked, with only a hint of sarcasm.

One of the things she liked best about the Captain was that beneath the trappings, he was a very practical man. "Leave me three," he told her, and so she counted out his three and then moved the rest to her work area near the porch.

By late afternoon, the milk crates were filled, the parts inventoried, and her new blue shirt was cool, crisp and holding up nicely.

"You need to eat," the Captain told her just as she was putting a stack of copper tubing away.

Once inside, the Captain poured her a glass of water and pushed back her hair, looking concerned, his usual expression. "You're red. I don't have any sunscreen. I should have thought about that."

Brooke put a hand to her warm cheeks. "I'll be fine."

He shook his head. "Stay inside for a while. I need to get some things from town. I'll be back."

She scanned the room, with its lack of standard living room accoutrements and it's odd hodge-podge order. Some might have called it haphazard, but by now she had seen into the Captain's hodge-podge brain, and there was never any haphazard at all. "What am I supposed to do here?"

"Lay down. Watch television."

None of which sounded appealing, so she nodded in agreement, watched him drive away and then immediately started to clean. Oh, sure, the sink was spic and span, the stove had never been used. Instead of dishes, the cabinets were lined with jars of nuts—and not the eating kind, either. There were rows and rows of Mason jars filled with screws and wires and tiny unidentified plastic pieces that, according to Google, were transistors.

With a heavy sigh, Brooke shut the cabinet doors. This was the Captain's home, and yes, it wasn't the way she would accessorize her home, but she respected his space.

Needing to do something, she decided to tackle the bedroom next, but the white cotton covers were straightened with military precision. There were no pictures, no books, an absolutely sterile environment—except for the metal sculpture in the corner. The piece was nearly two feet high, an assortment of rounded metal spheres, with two pipes on the sides, plastic tubing streaming from the top. She studied the placement of the screws, and eventually she knew what it was.

A female.

Oh.

For a long time she held the piece, the metal cold in her hands, but these weren't her things. Carefully she put the piece back where she found it, and turned to find the Captain had returned.

"I made it for Max," he volunteered before she could ask. "He was an old army buddy. It was a birthday present. A joke." He came over, pressed a small button she had overlooked and twin light beams shot from the two rounded spheres on the top.

"Oh," was all Brooke could say.

"It's an army thing."

"Very creative."

The Captain took the sculpture and put it in a box, setting it next to the doorway. "I should have mailed it a long time ago."

His face was missing the openness of before, and she missed it. "You don't have to hide this because of me," she said, pulling the sculpture back from the box, and then pressing the button, watching the twin red lights shoot from the woman's bosom. Smiling, she pressed the button again. "Did you name her?"

"No, she really is for Max."

And yes, she believed he had made the sculpture for Max, but... "When's his birthday?"

"Last month." The Captain shrugged, completely missing the obvious. "I've been busy."

Brooke put the sculpture in the box, suspecting that the Captain would mail it off tomorrow. "He'll be the only person in town who has one."

The Captain folded the lid, putting the sculpture firmly out of sight. "Anyway."

Curious, she sat on the bed and wiped her cheeks as if she was tired. "Didn't you ever make one for you?"

"I have Dog."

Hearing his name, Dog whirred into the room. "You could get a real dog," she suggested.

Soullessly he stared at her through his one good eye. "Why?"

"I've always wanted a dog, a fluffy puppy, probably three, and lots and lots of cats."

He sat down next to her. "You didn't have any growing up?"

"No. You?"

"We had one dog for...I don't know. It seemed like forever."

"What was his name?"

"Dog."

Brooke laughed and he smiled back. Then, with an absent shake of the head he stood. "Maybe I'll get another one. When I'm ready."

Realizing the moment had passed, Brooke stood, too, following him out of the room. "You know, I've been thinking about the hardware in the kitchen. Now, before you start to argue, hear me out..."

THE NEXT MORNING, Brooke woke up alone. Outside, she could hear the Captain whistling, the intermittent sound of a drill and birdsong. For a few minutes, she allowed herself to be lazy, to twist up in the sheets and bury her head in the Captain's pillow.

Here, in his bed, the scent of him surrounded her and comforted her. This was Texas, this was home. This odd combination of dusty land and fresh-cut wood and welded metal and burned scrambled eggs.

She hugged the pillow closer, breathing deeply of the other scent, the musky smell of sex.

Once again last night he had tried to sleep in the shed. Unfortunately, her face had gotten sunburned yesterday and she needed help applying cream to the afflicted areas. When she remembered his capable hands on her, her fingers skimmed over her breasts, and while there was the standard biological response, she didn't experience the same kick. The burning heat of his skin was missing, the earnest magic of his mouth. No matter how hard she closed her eyes, the bed was cold without him.

In Brooke's experience, nothing ever lasted very long and good memories should be stored away carefully, trotted out at bus stations or all-night diners, or when your employer decided that rubbing himself against you was romantic. There weren't many good memories in Brooke's life, and being with the Captain was the most decadent memory she'd ever kept.

Men usually didn't try to be good, but the Captain sure did. Every time he fought against his attraction, she only wanted him more. The hungry way he kissed her, as if he could never have enough. The way he touched her between the legs, the way his gaze grew so heavy as he watched her come. She slipped a finger inside herself, surprised by the throb, surprised by the ache. A void.

Hidden beneath the sheets she touched herself, pleasured herself, temporarily feeling a void she never knew she had. Faster and faster she stroked, finding a mechanical rhythm without hunger and life. Eventually the bubble inside her burst and her muscles shuddered and then relaxed.

Quickly she got out of bed and straightened the sheets. After cleaning up in the bathroom, she dressed for the day, but unfortunately, the void inside her remained.

THERE WAS BREAKFAST on the table. The Captain had attempted scrambled eggs. Next to the plate was an envelope with her name on it. Curious, Brooke drew out the single sheet of paper and twenty fifty-dollar bills. They seemed to be real. Not sure what to make of this, Brooke read over the invoice. Apparently the Captain was paying her for three days work, plus an advance against her salary.

At the bottom, in neat letters, he'd handwritten *Buy New Shoes*.

Brooke laughed and folded up the invoice, wondering who bought thousand-dollar shoes. However, she wasn't going to take his advance, only the money she'd earned. After removing one fifty and folding it in her pocket, she hid the other nineteen bills in a Mason jar in his cabinets, buried somewhere between oversize eye bolts and a Russian Geiger counter. Someday he'd find his money, but not today.

As soon as she hit the front porch, he pointed to a floppy hat that was hanging on the rail. "You need to wear that today."

The hat was too big, and the camouflage pattern wasn't something she would have chosen for herself. However, until she could buy something suitable, it'd do.

While she positioned the hat on her head, the Captain watched, frowning at the way it hung low in her eyes. He scratched his jaw, and then walked to the shed, returning a few seconds later with some sort of tool.

Without a word, he took off the hat, folded a pleat in the back and with one click, he'd adjusted the size perfectly.

When he returned the hat to her, she examined his work. "What is that?"

"Staple gun," he answered, and then after that he walked away.

A MORNING BREEZE WAS blowing in from the east, cooling the air. Brooke worked silently, but she noticed that the Captain wasn't doing his usual today. Long wooden boards had been pulled from the shed. He'd dug four small holes in the yard, filled them with cement, and then anchored in four wooden posts. However, Brooke chose not to ask, instead focusing on what apparently was a collection of antique medical instruments.

After lunch, the Captain dragged out a ladder and climbed up on the roof of the house. Fascinated, Brooke watched as he connected the boards from the top of the house to the posts, making some sort of frame.

Still, the Captain hadn't volunteered any information and Brooke decided that this was none of her business, and she'd worked on until the sun was low and red, looking like a ball of fire at the end of the world. The Captain continued, unwinding some sort of dark netting and then nailing it to the frame.

At sundown, Brooke went inside, typing in her notes on the Captain's computer. Two hours later, she could hear the hammering on the roof, and she worried that it was too dark to be safe. Deciding that prudence overcame privacy, she marched outside and found him on the roof.

Finally she had to ask. "What's going on?"

He climbed down from the ladder and dusted his hands. "Weatherproofing."

She examined the netting above her head. "For what?"

"It's something I should have put up a long time ago. Keeps off the heat. Keeps off the sun." With that, he gathered up his tools and went inside.

Brooke looked up, saw the moonlight and the stars streaming through like tiny dots of lights. All she could do was smile.

SOMETIME DURING THE DAY, the Captain had brought in an old dining-room table and chairs, or maybe he'd built them, she wasn't sure. There were frozen Salisbury steaks for dinner and Brooke made a mental note to drive into town and by food. Real food. Twenty-five dollars would go a long way toward some fruit and vegetables. When you were raised on breakfast cereal and soup, real food was very appealing.

Dog took away the dishes, and after Brooke curled up on the couch, he brought her a beer. The Captain had taken over the table, repairing a hand mixer, but Brooke decided there were questions she wanted to ask, questions she had a right to ask since they were about her family, her property and her future financial prosperity.

Although the Captain was studiously ignoring her, Brooke wasn't fooled. A person should be aware when they are the focus of attention—wanted, unwanted or otherwise. When she and her mother were living in a shelter in Cleveland, they had been robbed four times because Charlene Hart wasn't smart enough to know when she was the focus of unwanted attention. Then Brooke had taken over security, hiding their cash in her shoe, and the robberies had stopped. No, it was smart to always know.

The Captain always knew. She supposed that was the military background, which made sense because if Brooke wasn't alert, she might have been robbed—if the Captain wasn't alert, he might have been killed. Maybe someday she would ask about that, but for now, she felt like she needed to keep the conversation on more impersonal things.

"May I ask you something?"

He looked up, looked nervous, but nodded.

"I've noticed all the oil wells around here. Do you think they've found it all?"

"Probably." Apparently believing the conversation to be over, the Captain went back to his task.

"But Sonya doesn't believe that's true. Why does she think that?"

The Captain, apparently now realizing the conversation wasn't over, put down his screwdriver. "Look, I grew up in Baltimore, not Texas. I haven't lived out hre that long, but I've seen how the oil industry happens. Maybe they are doing some more work out here, but it's a crap shoot. Tin Cup is at the perimeter of some fields and every time that gasoline goes up, some greedy suits crawl out from their rock, hoping to make a buck."

He waited, hand poised over the screwdriver, and Brooke decided that she could find out her answers later.

Eventually, the Captain realized that she wasn't going to press him and returned his attention to the mixer.

Not wanting to disturb him, Brooke picked at the corner of his army trunk and thought how much nicer it would look if she painted it. Nothing very flashy, maybe a soft blue. She liked blue. After glancing at the Captain, she thought that maybe she'd ask next week.

He put down his screwdriver and looked up. She noticed that he didn't sigh. "They drill test wells, see what happens, lots of people show up, all sorts of rigs and machines, making a mess with no respect for the land."

Brooke nodded and the Captain went back to work.

A few seconds later he sighed and put down the screwdriver again. "It's not like she needs the money. She's a lawyer. I send her money. The house in Killeen is paid for. I don't get it."

He paused, apparently expecting Brooke to now take part in the conversation, which she did. "Maybe she wants it for you."

"I don't need anything."

"I know."

The Captain went back to finishing the mixer, next pulling out a board with wires and lights and switches, but apparently he wasn't happy with that. He swore and looked up. "Why'd you ask?"

"Austen's place isn't far from here. I was thinking how cool it would be if there was oil on the Hart land. I mean,

I don't care about being rich or anything, but...it'd be nice. We could build a house, maybe have a garden. Curtains. Blue curtains, I think."

The Captain stopped what he was doing and studied her, his mouth a hard line. "I should have told you this earlier because you should know that Austen's involved with another woman, and I think you should leave him alone."

6

WORDS WERE DANGEROUS THINGS, which was why Jason never used a lot of them. He would have liked to blame Brooke's red face on sunburn, but he wasn't a stupid man, and the aloe vera that he'd rubbed all over last night had really done the trick.

"Either that is the most disgusting idea that anyone has ever thought about me, or else you think I've traveled across half the continental United States on the basis of some delusional family. So, please tell me, Captain, am I an incestuous sleaze or a crazy lady? And you can only pick one."

Jason opened his mouth, thought better of it, and shut it again. She was steaming mad, which he found disgustingly arousing, but he knew that he had to man up and admit the truth.

"If Austen is really your brother, then why the hell are you broke and living in your car?"

It was another mistake. Her eyes filled with tears and Jason hated to see a woman cry, and this was Brooke, who, as he had just told her, was broke and living in her car.

She didn't answer, not that he expected her to. Instead, he watched her stomp to the door, open the door, stop, slam the door, go back to the bedroom, emerge with his pillow, open the door, stop, and then she glared at him.

"Your money's in the jar. I don't need it." The door slammed, and Brooke was gone.

Furiously, Jason swore, picked up the circuit board and threw it across the room, watching the tiny pieces scatter across the floor.

A long time ago, he would have known what to do. A long time ago, he would have been better able to think on his feet. A long time ago, he wouldn't have been so far off the mark.

A long time ago, it wouldn't have hurt so bad.

Brooke didn't like feeling stupid, she didn't like feeling small. She didn't like being broke, and she didn't like living in her car.

The front seat was too cramped, she noted, bashing her knees on the steering wheel for the eighteenth time, her goose-feathered duvet smelled like French fries instead of burned scrambled eggs, but the pillow smelled exactly like the Captain.

She should have been smarter. She should have known better, but all the *shouldas* didn't help.

Furious with herself, she kicked at the door, tossing this way and that to find a more comfortable position.

The Captain tapped on the window and she ignored him.

"I'm sorry."

"Go away."

"Brooke, you can't sleep in the car."

"I belong in the car. Go away."

"You don't belong in the car."

"I don't belong in the house."

"I can't leave you out here like this."

"You don't have to take care of crazy people."

"You're not crazy. Come in the house."

"No."

"At least talk to me."

"I am."

"In the house."

"No."

She heard him try the handle, but the doors were locked. Car doors should always be locked.

After a few minutes he left, and Brooke was alone. She should be happy that she was alone. She should be happy that the Captain had given up. She was so happy, she kicked at the door. It hurt just as badly as before, but the pain in her foot was better than the pain in her head.

There was a click and then the back door creaked open, and the Captain climbed in her car.

"I don't want you in my car."

"Technically, your car is on my property."

"I can park somewhere else."

"I'm sorry, Brooke. I'm very, very sorry."

The sincerity in his voice ripped at her heart, and she knew that was the best and worst thing about the Captain. If he saw a person in a hole, he needed to pull them out, but sometimes a person needed to crawl out of the hole themselves. Brooke didn't want him to see her as a hole-dweller. She wanted him to see her as a desirable woman, and she knew that some of the time he did.

Right now, with her feelings so raw, she wanted to hear him say it, wanted him to admit that he wanted her. It wasn't very nice of her because he would never tell her that, although it meant he could be as silent and therefore as miserable as her at least.

The silence grew, filling the car until Brooke kicked at the door. "Get out."

"You can sleep in the house, or I can sleep out here. You pick."

In answer, Brooke kicked the door once again.

THE MORNING SUN HIT Jason in the eyes, and he twisted his neck, a hairbrush stabbing him in the face. Three times he stretched, but the knots in his body remained.

In a lot of ways, Jason knew the situation was for the best. Brooke should have gone to her brother right away. Idiot.

From the front seat, he could hear her soft breathing and knew she was still fast asleep. If he closed his good eye he could forget the stack of magazines under his knee, he could forget the duct-taped seat cushion and forget the hurt in her eyes.

If he closed his good eye, he could see her welcoming him in his bed, remember the way she felt in his arms.

But sex was a dangerous drug. Brooke was a dangerous drug so Jason opened his one good eye and climbed out of her car, the door creaking like an old woman's knee. Her breathing caught, and he knew she was awake, but she didn't say a word, not that he expected her to.

As he walked toward his house, he didn't look back. He heard the sound of her engine, the sound of her wheels on the drive and, soon enough, Jason's life was restored to the same place it'd been before.

BROOKE FOLLOWED the map to the Hart homestead, excitement roiling in her stomach. This was her home, the place where Charlene and Frank Hart had lived together in bitter matrimony. She'd put off this part of the journey, the last part, out of fear. She had wanted the meeting with Austen to be perfect, but since Brooke had very little experience with perfection, she now recognized the flaw in her plan.

The Captain hadn't thought she was capable. No, the Captain thought she was certifiable. Excitement changed to a hollow emptiness, and she got angry with him all over again. However, today was for new beginnings and she made herself smile at the bright, sunshiny day.

A new start with a new brother, a new home, and what did the Captain know, after all?

After she took the last turn onto Orchard Drive, she drove two long miles seeing nothing but trees and grass. When she finally spied the house, she stopped, stared. Frowned.

There was no picket fence, no charming garden, no bounding dog. Frankly, as a home, it lacked just about everything.

There was a man and a woman working on the house, actually it seemed more like demolition than renovation. Considering the condition of the place, demolition seemed optimal. Her brother, Austen Hart, was swinging a sledge hammer, destroying one of the two interior walls that still remained. A very pretty, stylish woman was using a chain saw to slice through some rusted out pipes.

Welcome home, Brooke, she thought, and then laughed at herself. She'd seen worse, she'd survived.

After she parked the old Impala, Brooke climbed out, prepared to see her brother. Hopefully he would remember who she was. "Austen! It's Brooke! Your sister," she added, mainly as a reminder.

Austen put down the hammer, the chain saw shut off, and Brooke made her way past what was left of the porch steps. The woman looked her over, and Brooke wished she'd taken the Captain's advice and sprung for new boots.

"I'm his sister. Brooke Hart." She held out a friendly hand. "Very pleased to meet you."

The woman shook her hand, and Brooke noticed her

fabulous nails and tried not to be jealous. "Gillian Wanamaker."

With the back of his sleeve, Austen wiped the sweat from his brow, but didn't offer his hand until Gillian Wanamaker nudged him in the side.

Instead of shaking her hand, her brother pulled her into a hug, and it was the world's most awkward hug. Brooke knew this because she had experienced more than her fair share of awkward hugs, some wanted, some not.

"I didn't know you were coming to visit. Hell, we would've put out a welcome mat." Austen glanced toward the house and laughed. It was an awkward laugh. "What are you doing in town?"

"I came to see the house," Brooke told him. *And maybe stay forever.* Austen walked her through the remains, and she wondered what it had been like when her mother and father had lived there. When Austen and Tyler had lived there.

"Not much to see right now. It's a work in progress. The old structure was condemned and the lawyer gave me the green light to tear down the place."

Gillian pointed to a freshly poured slab in the distance. "The new house is going up over there." Then her attention returned to Brooke. "Austen didn't mention where you lived, or maybe he did, but in this whole getting-married hoo-doo, it probably slipped my mind."

"I'm from New York," Brooke answered, then nodded to the house. "It looks great."

"Have you talked to the lawyer?" asked Austen. "He was trying to track you down."

"That's why I came, but he's out of town. Do you know what he wants?" Brooke asked, trying to sound casual.

Austen began to laugh. "This is your inheritance."

Brooke swallowed. "I'm in the will? My father knew about me?"

Austen shook his head. "The state executed the will last spring because you have a legal claim and it's only right that you get your share. We're sitting on four acres, so you get one-third of that and one-third of the house.

"One-third of the house?" asked Brooke, trying to look excited.

Austen wasn't fooled and he laughed, and she liked to hear him laugh. "It doesn't work that way," he explained. "Once you sign the papers, I'll write you a check for the cash equivalent. I should warn you, it's not a lot, probably nothing more than a couple of haircuts for you."

Brooke wasn't disappointed. Much. A couple of New York haircuts went a long, long way. It'd keep her in peanut butter until she could find a new job. And maybe she could spring for a motel room.

"And one-third of the mineral rights," Gillian added, which perked Brooke up. Certainly the house wasn't what she was expecting, but still, one-third of something was infinitely preferable to one-third of nothing. She was about to ask her brother more when he noticed the Impala parked at the end of the road. "You drove from New York, or is that a rental?"

"I borrowed it from a friend," Brooke told him because she could see he didn't approve of the car's ramshackle condition.

"Must have been some friend."

"What do you do in New York?" Gillian asked, smiling at her, not nearly as awkwardly. "It must be so exciting."

"I, uh…" began Brooke, not wanting to lie, because this was her fresh start, and she wanted to make the right imprssion, but…

"She works for an art gallery," Austen replied.

"I quit that job," Brooke stated quickly.

"You're in art?" Gillian asked, and Brooke knew that she was going to have to give some sort of response, but her already frayed nerves were starting to go, and the sun was very hot, and this wasn't going nearly as easily as she'd planned, and Gillian was watching her with concern.

"You're looking really pale. I bet you're not used to this weather." Gillian glanced at Austen and clucked her tongue. "You don't look so good, either, sugar. You know, let's ditch this place and go somewhere hospitable to chat. I've got some chocolate cake at my place. Are you hungry? I don't mean to brag, but it's the best thing you've ever tasted."

Then Gillian Wanamaker grabbed Austen's hand, linking them together, and Brooke approved and the panic faded. "Come on, sweetie. We need to show this one how real family is done."

THE WANAMAKER HOUSE was far more in line with what Brooke considered a home. Needlework pillows covered the sofa, family pictures hung from the wall, and from the kitchen came the smell of warm chocolate cake. It was the perfect place for Brooke to get to know her brother better. And hopefully he would want to know her as well, not that she was making any progress there, judging by the closed expression on his face. However, if ever there was a place that would make a non-family a family, the Wanamaker household was it.

Gillian's mother, Modine Wanamaker, was a plump maternal type with a flour-dusted apron and a welcoming smile.

Emmett Wanamaker was a man of few words, as apparently were most of the men in Tin Cup. He finished his cake, pushed back from the dining room table and fled for the football game in the other room. Austen appeared to want to join him, but Gillian stopped him with a look.

As Brooke finished the last crumbs of her cake, she put down her fork and smiled at her brother, who smiled warily back. "Congratulations on your engagement. I love the ring, and I imagine the wedding is going to be fabulous."

At the mention of his fiancée, some of the wariness disappeared, and Brooke mentally patted herself on the back. Apparently all the Harts were romantics.

"I'm lucky to have her," he said, taking Gillian's hand, his feelings apparent on his face.

"When's the big day?"

"Middle of November."

"Will you be living in the new house or here? This is such a nice place." Brooke ran her finger over the embroidered chair rests. She'd never learned how to create such beautiful things, and she had always wanted to, but it seemed frivolous unless she had a wall to hang it, on a sofa to throw it over or a chair to decorate. Like this one.

"Originally the new house was going to be for Gillian's parents," Austen said, "and we were going to live here, but then Gillian and I decided that a new place would be good."

"This is Gillian's house," Modine explained.

"Don't explain, Mama." Gillian smiled at Brooke. "Our housing situation has always been complicated."

Brooke nodded because she understood that. Still, this was like the best of all worlds. It had the feel of family, of home, of love. Austen must have had that at the old house, as well. "I'm sure you had some wonderful memories growing up."

"Not a single one, but all that's going to change." Austen met her eyes, and she saw the determination there. Romantic and fool-hardy. Brooke found herself liking her brother more and more.

"So tell me what you're doing now?" Brooke asked, and for the next half hour, Austen told her about his life. He talked about his job for the railroad commissioner, helping out on her campaign for governor and keeping an eye on construction of the new rail line through the town. He bragged about Gillian's contributions to the town, he talked about Tyler and his surgical advances in New York, but not a word about the house on Orchard Lane, or Frank Hart. No questions about Charlene Hart at all, which was probably for the best since Brooke didn't like to speak ill of her mother. Brooke had lied to her brother once, and she wasn't happy about the idea of lying again.

"Now that you've heard the Austen Hart saga, how about you? When I saw you in New York, you were getting married, too, weren't you?"

Sadly, Brooke shook her head. "It wasn't meant to be." True love couldn't be bought or rented for two hundred dollars an hour. "I think we were at different places in our lives. Different dreams. Different goals." Peter, her pretend fiancé had wanted her to pay for a cozy hotel suite at the Plaza. Brooke merely wanted to make a good impression on her brothers.

Gillian nodded. "I know. You can't fill out some application and get love made to order. You fall when you fall."

Her mother clucked her tongue, then began clearing away the dishes. "I knew Junior was all wrong for you."

After her mother bustled from the kitchen, Gillian looked at Brooke apologetically. "I'd love to have you bunk here, but we're overflowing as it as. Mom and Dad moved in with me a few years ago, and they have the guest room, and Austen takes the couch, and I can't ask you to sleep on the floor. Once the construction on the new house is finished, we'll move in there and let Mama and Daddy take over this place. Hopefully they won't decide to give this one away, either."

"I wasn't expecting to intrude..." Brooke started, but then Gillian interrupted.

"There's a nice little hotel just down the road. The Spotlight Inn. Tell Delores you're family, and she'll treat you right."

Brooke thought of the fifty ⌐ollars in her pocket and wondered if the family discount would be enough. Better to save her money for more important things. Like gas, or food. Not wanting to complain, she managed a smile. "The Spotlight Inn sounds lovely. I'll check in tonight."

IT WAS THIRTY MINUTES of courteous chit-chat, before Gillian found the opportunity to drag her fiancé into the living room, without seeming rude.

"Now, Austen," Gillian said, using her most patient voice. She loved this man dearly, but at some point in their relationship, he would need to start telling her things. "I know you think I'm just some dizzy-headed blonde, in spite of the fact that I'm the duly elected sheriff of this town, and have spent the last five years keeping it afloat. Not that any of that is important, mind you, because I would be a very small-minded woman if I let such thoughts wound my pride. However, during the last seven months we've been together, we've made sacred promises to each other. We are to be married in a mere forty-five days because we have created a relationship based on trust and honesty. And yes, you have explored my body more intimately than any gynecologist ever could. As such, I am deserving of the truth. A sister? Sweetie, as far as deep, dark secrets of your past, a sister is the least of your concerns. A sister is family, a blood relation, a woman who shared your mother's womb."

Austen's face squared into what Gillian termed his

stubborn look. "I didn't grow up with her, Gillian. She cruised some all-American life, and yes, we share some DNA, but she's pretty much a stranger. I don't know squat about her."

Glancing toward the closed door to the kitchen, Gillian was glad she had insisted on extra insulation for the house, but since she didn't believe in leaving anything to chance, she set her voice to a whisper. "And you won't know anything unless you talk to her."

"You're going to make me do this?"

"Don't you want a sister?"

"No. I have one brother, and it took me nearly twenty-five years to understand that one. Besides," he grabbed her hand and his eyes went all dark and moonstruck, "you're my family, Gilly. You're my heart, my soul, my blood. How am I supposed to have room in my heart for anyone else?"

Her eyes narrowed. "Romantic talk will not relieve you of your familial obligations. Why, if you gave her half a chance, you might end up liking her."

Austen glanced at the door, glanced at Gillian, then sighed. "All right, but did you see the car? She's got money, her stepfather was some save-the-world preacher and, Mom—goddammit, Mom turned into one of those mothers who makes homemade soup and wears aprons."

And then Gillian understood. On the outside, Austen was some big macho doofus, but on the inside, he was just a little boy who'd had his mother stolen away. She wrapped her arms around him, soothing wounds that would never heal. "Your mother left the best part of the Hart family behind."

"Except for Frank."

"Except for Frank, but in spite of your mother's bad decision-making skills, I don't think Brooke has had such an easy time of it."

He pressed a warm kiss on her hair. "You're just saying that to make me like her."

"Did you see her boots?"

"No."

"Austen, those boots looked like something the dogs had chewed up and spit out. She needs a family. She needs a brother. She needs a home."

"You know all this because of your top-notch investigative skills?"

Gillian smiled. "Call it women's intuition."

He laughed, slid a familiar hand down her backside and squeezed. "What's your women's intuition telling you now?"

Her hips moved forward in a frankly provocative invitation, but true love would not be denied. "Sneak into my room later, and we'll discuss it in extensive detail."

Austen heaved an extravagant sigh. "Tell me that someday we'll be able to share a bed for the entire night. It's like I'm sixteen all over again."

She patted the Texas Longhorn beneath his fly and then moved away, before they were doing it on the sofa again. Having herself, her parents and Austen all living under one roof was a painful exercise in delayed sexual gratification, but Gillian knew that once they were married, these days of stolen quickies and shared showers would be behind her.

Before she could leave the living room, Austen snagged her by the waist and pulled her close for a deep kiss.

THE WEEKEND PASSED like the world's longest hangover but Jason hadn't touched a drop. Normally, he lost himself in the art of repair, or a drive to San Angelo where he would inspect the scrap yards for whatever caught his eye. Or maybe he would call his father, say hello to the old man and listen to him rail about the Orioles or his property tax bill or his most recent trip to the doc.

Not this time.

It weighed on Jason's conscience, not knowing that she was okay. He had assumed the worst about her, and he'd been wrong. Now she was back out there alone.

He was a moron.

His conscience wasn't going to shut up until he knew she was sleeping safely under somebody's roof. Somebody that wouldn't take advantage of her—like he had, he reminded himself, which only made his conscience holler more.

By Monday morning, he spurred himself to action. For Jason this meant driving into town and wandering aimlessly until he could discover some answers.

It took him thirty-seven minutes to discover that he wasn't a good aimless wanderer, and no matter how hard he tried, he couldn't do casual.

Blame it on the military.

At the Hinkle's, he picked up some eggs and milk. At Zeke's Auto Garage he ordered a new air filter. At Dot's, he bought himself a cup of coffee, and read the *Tin Cup Gazette*. After reading a four-page account of the Friday night bingo game where Father Louis banned Emmaline Herzog for cheating, Jason remembered why he didn't like the *Tin Cup Gazette*.

Once his cup of coffee was empty, he took a long, hard look at his purchases, and donated the milk and eggs to Dot. In the future, he would know that perishables were the last to be bought, not the first.

At the First National Bank and Trust, he opened another safety deposit box, walking away with a brand-new coffee maker as part of some promotional event. The library had a closed sign in the window, so he proceeded to the town hall to find out if he had any unpaid parking tickets.

For six freaking hours, Jason wandered the four streets that made up downtown Tin Cup, in the process learning several things. Brooke's brother was not getting coffee or buying groceries or cashing a check at the bank or chatting with the sheriff at the Town Hall. If Brooke's brother was going to turn unsociable, why did he have to pick this day to start?

But then, as the afternoon sun was starting to fade, Jason finally spotted the elusive Austen Hart exiting the post office.

Jason plotted his strategy, deciding that if he walked east on Main, backtracked up 17, he could probably duck into the feed store and bump into Hart on the way out.

Everything worked exactly right. Jason exited the store, taking a position in front of Hart, then halting abruptly.

"Whoa, sorry. You okay?" the man asked after he'd run into Jason, which was what Jason wanted, but he still felt like a moron. Oh, yeah, because he was.

Absently, Jason rubbed his shoulder, which didn't hurt, but at least it was something to do. "Fine." Then he scanned the streets, frowning. "You know where I could get a twelve-volt battery?"

Austen laughed. "Not here." He held out his hand, one of those good ole boy sort of shakes. "Austen Hart."

"Jason Kincaid. I don't get into town much. You live around here?"

"At my fiancée's house for the moment. I own a place that should've been condemned by the county. It's going to take some time to fix. You?"

"Five miles west on County Road 163."

"The old Hinkle place? That property runs up to mine. That's you?"

At Jason's nod, Hart continued, a lot chattier than Jason

could ever be. "We're neighbors. After we get it fixed up, we'll have you over, throw some steaks on the grill."

"We?" Jason asked, taking the opening, running with it. "You have family here?"

"Gillian's my fiancée. She's the sheriff," Hart answered, which wasn't what Jason had hoped to hear.

"Nice to have connections."

"Sometimes I speed, just so she can cuff me," Hart said with a friendly laugh.

The man was easy to like, knew how to converse with anybody, but he said nothing about Brooke. Jason racked his brain for impromptu conversation, but Dog's limited vocabulary skills meant that Jason was out of practice. "Not a big town. You grew up here?"

"Me and my brother. Don't believe what you hear. Long story."

Another opening. Steer it back to the family.

"You know, I would've killed to have a brother. It was me and my little sister, and she was always tailing after me. Eventually she grew out of it, but not soon enough. Know what I mean?" The story wasn't true. Jason had five brothers and one sister, Sara, who was still in Baltimore. Sara had never followed any of the Kincaid brothers around, but creating some sort of friendly rapport was Jason's last shot at interrogation. At first he thought he'd blown it, but then Hart nodded like he agreed.

"It's good you know your sister. Mine just showed up on my doorstep this week. Up until last year, we didn't even know she existed. Now that she's here, I'm as clueless as a pig wearing a watch."

At least that was some progress. Jason shot him a sympathetic look. "Families are a true pain in the ass. That's why you're in town? Escaping all that estrogen at your fiancée's?"

Hart shook his head. "Brooke—that's my sister—isn't staying with us. The house is packed as it is, so Brooke took a room at the Spotlight. The inn's not real fancy, but at least this way she gets her own bed and doesn't have to wait in line for the shower. Mornings are killer at the Wanamaker house."

Jason smiled stupidly, but inside he was seething. He knew that Brooke wasn't at the Spotlight Inn. No, she'd be homesteading it in her car, parked on some desolate part of the highway, a target for overzealous cops or where serial killers could happen upon her.

After a fast check at his watch, Jason pretended to be rattled, not hard since he was still seeing red. "Look at that! Four o'clock. Time flies, doesn't it. Listen, it was great to meet you. I'll see you around."

With that, Jason set out on a search-and-rescue mission. Hopefully Brooke would see things in a practical manner and come home.

Probably not. Bring the heat, bring the stupid. It was the Army way.

Brooke didn't want to be happy to see the Captain. She didn't want to be relieved when his truck popped into view, but she was. When she watched his long body climb out of the cab, she felt a heavy weight lift from her shoulders.

Weakness and knotted muscles, nothing more, she told herself, still mad that he'd misjudged her. It wasn't relief, but the heat of the sun making her dizzy. As he approached her car, she schooled her features into appropriate disapproval.

The Captain opened the driver's-side door and scowled. "You could have come back."

Brooke snorted. "I'm the crazy lady, remember? The

flaky little nympho who chases men across the country because I looove them."

The scowl deepened. "I'm sorry."

"Your apologies would mean a lot more if you didn't keep screwing up. You should move back from the door. You're blocking my view."

"Why didn't you tell your brother you couldn't afford the hotel?"

"Would you tell your family that you couldn't afford a hotel? Would you tell your family if there was a problem? And don't even think about lying to me, because I know you better than that."

"Hart seems like a nice guy. He'd understand."

Of course he'd understand. Everyone would understand. And she would be branded as the Incapable One for life. No, thank you. Brooke lifted her chin. "Once the lawyer returns and the paperwork is signed, Austen is going to buy me out."

The Captain pulled his cap off his head, pushed it back, and she could see the frustration in his eyes. "And what are you going to do until then?"

"I'll find a job, If I can't find one here, I'll go to Houston, or Dallas. There's a job for me somewhere."

The frustration in his face faded and gentled into something that made her dizzy again. "Your brother isn't in Houston or Dallas. Your home isn't in Houston or Dallas. You already have a job here. Come back to the house."

"Why should I go with you?" she asked, wanting to hear the words. Wanting to hear him say that he wanted her, that he needed her, and it scared her how badly she ached to hear those words.

Mutely he stared. Patiently she waited.

Finally, he pointed to the old abandoned farmhouse she'd

parked behind. "You can't live in your car. You could get killed."

Brooke wanted to scream. Instead, she smiled sweetly. "Your concern for my safety is touching, but unnecessary. I've been doing great in my car. That's the pleasant thing about inanimate objects. Unlike I do with human beings, I don't expect them to care." She tried to pull the door closed, but the Captain was not only animate, but immoveable. *Darn it.*

"You won't come back?" he asked, a blinding glimpse of the obvious.

"No."

He scanned the horizon, rubbed his jaw thoughtfully. "There's laws against public vagrancy. I can tell the Sheriff. Imagine how she would feel knowing that her future sister-in-law lives in a car."

No!

Brooke pounded on the steering wheel, wishing it were his head. "You wouldn't dare."

The Captain only smiled.

He would dare. He was that way.

Brooke closed her eyes, blocking out his image, blocking out the shabby inside of her car. The Impala wasn't supposed to be home. He was supposed to believe her. Austen should have welcomed her with open arms.

Brooke felt the pain deep in her soul, felt it work through her, and then let it pass. Her world had never been what it was supposed to be, and sometimes, late in the night, she worried that it never would.

Tired, sore and spent, she opened her eyes and saw the Captain waiting for his answer. There was dust on his boots, his jaw was locked and the single gray eye was the color of iron.

In answer, Brooke pulled back her hair, tightened her

jaw and met his gaze evenly. "Don't think I will let you touch me." Even as she said the words, she knew it was a lie.

"I wouldn't expect you to. To be honest, it'll be a lot easier. Things won't get messed up. Take your job back. I'll sleep in the shed. The pay will be the same and, in return, I keep quiet."

And no, even when blackmailing her, he still had to be the gentleman.

"I won't let you sleep in the shed. It's wrong."

His eyes flickered toward her. The steel turned into heat. "Don't go there, Brooke."

"Take the couch," she clarified. She hated this. Hated that she could never be a guest, only a burden.

"No."

The wind kicked in, the smell of dust, dirt and defeat. "Please. This is hard enough."

"Why is that? Why is it so hard for you to accept random acts of kindness?"

Her shoulders slumped because, in the end, Brooke would never be as strong as she wanted, never be as smart as she wanted. She wiped at the final humiliation—her own tears. "Take the couch. Please."

For an endless moment, the Captain stood over her, strong and silent, but in the end, he slammed the car door and swore.

Slowly, Brooke repaired her face, shored up the cracks in her dignity and then followed the Captain's truck home.

7

THE GOLD-LETTERED SIGN OVER the doorway said "Hiram Hadley, Esquire," but it might as well have said "Brooke's Future—Enter Here." Without knowing it, Austen had given her the best present ever—hope. With the money that her brother was going to give her for her inheritance, she'd have a down payment on a place to call home. This was her chance for the Captain to see her as someone valuable, too. People very rarely saw Brooke as someone valuable.

In Detroit she gotten by on a grocery clerk's salary until the store had closed. In Minnesota she had waitressed in a bar, until the manager had kept her late one evening and explained her new job resonsibilites, which involved her mouth meeting his penis. She introduced her knee to his balls, and decided that St. Paul wasn't the place for her. Brooke had spent the last ten years moving from place to place, looking for a spot to belong, but for the first time, Brooke didn't want to leave, she wanted to stay, but on her own terms, on her own two feet.

Briskly she knocked at the door, but alas, Brooke's future was not answering.

In case Mr. Hadley had returned and was hard of hearing, Brooke knocked harder. "Hello! Is anyone in there?"

"Good golly, missy. Can you stop the hammering? Even my cat is getting anxious."

Slowly she lowered her arm and turned, finding the dry cleaner, a pudgy man with a balding, bullet-shaped head, scowling at her. However, contrary to his statement, his cat was definitely not anxious. The round animal was winding his way through Brooke's ankles, rolling on the cement steps, belly-flopping one way then the other. Brooke reached down and petted the more forgiving feline. "I'd like to speak to Mr. Hadley."

"He's in North Dakota."

"Well, yes, I know that."

"Then why are you knocking on his door?"

Brooke rose and held out her hand. "I'm Brooke Hart. You're the dry cleaner? I've heard you do very good work."

Grudgingly he shook her hand, kerosene-like fumes drifting to Brooke's nose. "Arnold Cervantes. If you need something cleaned, I'm your man. But I still don't get it. If you know Hiram's gone, then why are you here?"

His tone wasn't very nice, but Brooke reminded herself to remain friendly. If she worked with those chemicals all day, she wouldn't be a happy person, either. "Doesn't anyone else work in the office?"

"Lizzie's his secretary."

"Why isn't she answering the door?" Brooke asked, which she thought was a very logical question.

"She's in Dallas while Hiram's taking care of his dad. He gave her the time off. Seemed silly for her to sit in the office and twiddle her thumbs while he's gone. Why're you so all-fired to talk to Hiram?"

"I have some legal matters with my brother that need to be arranged. It's regarding the Hart property. Mr. Hadley called me."

"Why didn't you call him back?"

"He doesn't have an answering machine."

The man began to laugh.

"This isn't funny," Brooke told him, deciding that pretend-friendly had gone on long enough. "I drove a long way to talk to Mr. Hadley and everybody here thinks it's normal that his office is shut down."

Looking somewhat ashamed, the dry cleaner blew out a breath. "Sorry, missy. Give me your name and a phone number and I'll call his father's place."

"You could just give me the number and I'll save you the trouble," Brooke suggested, not wanting to admit that she didn't have a phone and not exactly sure that Mr. Cervantes would do it anyway.

The man picked up his unhappily mewing cat. "You know those trusting folks who believe everybody is who they say they are and want to chat all day on the phone?"

"Yes."

"Hiram's not one of them. Got to check everybody out. Probably why he went into law. Give me your name and number and I'll call him tonight. If it's an emergency, I'm sure he'd fly back and take care of matters, seeing as he's left you in a lurch and all."

An emergency? Was this an emergency? It wasn't like Brooke didn't have a roof over her head now. The Captain's roof, and yes, there were a lot of issues to be worked out between them, but Brooke fully intended to work them out, because no matter how mad he made her, he also made her feel safe and relaxed and desired. Most important of all, there had been times when she saw respect in his eyes. She'd had moments in her life when she was safe or relaxed or desired, but never respected—unless she was pretending to be someone who she wasn't, but with the Captain she didn't have to pretend.

No, this was no emergency. "I can wait until he gets back. I don't have a phone."

"I think what we have ourselves is a failure to communicate, missy," the man said, laughing again. She didn't think he was laughing at her, and she decided the Mr. Cervantes wasn't as bad as she had assumed. However, the fat cat in his arms was staring at her, not respecting her, because once again, Brooke was letting the door to her future close. No, not today.

"Wait." She wrote down her name and put the Captain's phone number after it. "This is my work number."

Mr. Cervantes adjusted the cat, freeing one hand, and then tucked the number in his pocket. "I'll pass it along and tell him it's an emergency."

"No!" she yelled, and now Mr. Cervantes was staring as well as the cat. "I mean, it's not a huge emergency. I get anxious sometimes. I should learn to relax more. It's why I moved out here. I lived in New York once."

"New York, huh? Pretty fancy place. You're going to find out we do things a lot different out here."

Brooke smiled at the man, because everything about this town was different, and that was exactly why it felt like home.

AFTER DINNER, Brooke watched Dog clear the dishes, noticing that this time, there were no glitches or flaws in the mechanical grips. Every time the Captain found something off, he had to repair it. Including her life. But she could repair her life first. If the mineral rights on the Hart land turned into real dollars... If the Captain could see her as something more than a mechanical automaton to be repaired. If only he could see her as a woman again.

If only...

From across the room, the Captain sat at the table,

tinkering with a gutted radio, studiously avoiding talking to her. Not that she wanted him to, but the silence between them had changed from something companionable to a war zone, and she wished he could repair the glitches in their relationship, as well. Not happy with the status quo, Brooke stood, preferring the lonely security of his bedroom to this.

"Brooke."

She stopped, turned. "Is this work related?"

He looked at her impassively, scarred and patched, a man who had suffered a lot more than her. "Please" was all he said, but that small conversation was better than nothing at all. Brooke snagged a barstool, pulling it close to his chair. Her foolish hands itched to straighten the screwdrivers or stroke the rough stubble at his jaw. Instead she folded them tightly in her lap.

"How are things with your brother? He's nice to you?"

They were conversing formally, like an employee and boss. Whatever. Brooke met his eye, equally cool. "Austen is nice enough. I like Gillian. They invited me to dinner tomorrow evening, so you won't be burdened with my company. Feel free to roll out the keg and strippers."

"You're usually nicer than this."

"I know. I felt like being catty."

The corner of his mouth lifted and she remembered the feel of his lips on her neck, the taste of him on her tongue. Her gaze drifted to the hefty ridge beneath his fly and stayed there. He knew. The air was charged with the tension, her overheated nerves sparking, nipples on alert. When he leaned closer, Brooke held her breath, but then the mulish Captain pulled back. "You should take the money and stay at the Inn." His voice was as rough and hard as his resolve.

"I'll only take what I earn," answered Brooke, because she could be just as stubborn.

He didn't look happy, but obviously he knew better than to argue. "All right," he agreed, turning back to his work, and she told herself she didn't care.

At the dismissal, she climbed down from the stool, acting the perfect employee and the perfect guest. "We're done?"

He picked up his screwdriver, pretending to work. Brooke knew better. The Captain's twists were always properly seated, never a wasted movement, much like when he was inside her. Not liking the direction of her thoughts, she looked away. "Do you need any clothes or female things?" he asked politely.

"No, thank you."

"Did you talk to the lawyer?"

"He's out of town."

"When is he coming back?"

"I don't know," she answered, and finally he looked up.

"Nobody has a phone number for him?"

Brooke shrugged. "I'm handling the situation. You don't need to be concerned."

She was surprised when his screwdriver tapped against a metal plate. The Captain wasn't a tapper. "I can be concerned."

"Everything is fine. When he comes back, I'll collect my money, take a room at the Spotlight Inn and I'll be out of your hair forever."

"I don't mind you staying here. I like you staying here, Brooke."

"Why?"

At her question, his scowl deepened, hard grooves cutting into his face. Realizing she wasn't going to get an answer, Brooke gestured to the couch. "Do you have an extra pillow and sheet? You'll need them."

"Are you going to give me my pillow back?"

She chose to ignore the question. "If the sheets are in the bedroom, you should get them now." There was an invitation in her voice that irked her, as if all she wanted was some sign that the Captain wanted to be in her bed again. One look, anything...

But, no.

"Get some rest. I'll see you in the morning," he said.

All night she watched the clock on the bedroom wall, wishing the time would move on. The bed was big and empty without him, and to make matters worse, she could hear him restless on the couch. Her feet wanted to go to him. She wanted to curl up beside him, but that wouldn't solve anything. From the other room, she could hear him mumble and swear because the couch wasn't long enough, and his feet were hanging over the side. His head would be cramped against the armrest, which, if she returned his pillow, wouldn't be a problem.

But the pillow stayed and Brooke lay there, uncomfortable in her own guilt. If he had come to bed, she would have melted like chocolate in the sun, but he didn't, and so Brooke pulled the pillow close and breathed in his scent.

Sadly, it wasn't enough.

THE DESIGN OF THE HOUSE didn't necessitate Jason passing by the bedroom to take a shower, but there he was, lurking in the doorway, watching her sleep. Bare shoulders poked out from under the covers, and he was grateful for the early morning chill in the air that kept her safely beneath the sheets.

In fact, as she snuggled deeper in the bed, he was feeling pretty good about the situation. There was nothing in the cloud of dark hair that would ink sexual fantasies on his brain. Nothing indecent in the graceful curve of her neck. In fact, if he wanted to, he could have stood there all day without getting turned on. Of course, then he'd officially be a stalker, which was a helluva lot creepier than just some guy with a hard-on, because 24/7, most men had hard-ons. It was the nature of the beast. Look at a cloud. See a woman's breasts surrounded by an elephant. Hard-on.

Wait for paint to dry, imagine long, stocking-encased legs hidden in the glossy swirls. Hard-on.

And yet, he thought proudly, here he was, watching her—most likely nude because she wasn't shy—and he was flaccid, limp, not even a drop of blood heading in the wrong direction.

Then she rolled over, and her arm slipped underneath the pillow. She had wonderfully sensual arms. Thin, but not toothpicks. There was muscle on Brooke Hart, more than she knew. When he had been on top of her, and her eyes were so aware, those sensual arms had locked him close. Her sleek thighs had wrapped around his hips, soldering them together...

Brooke sighed, her breathing deep and even, and Jason swore silently because his cock stood out like Pinocchio's nose, just as long, just as wooden, just as stupid.

It wasn't fair. There was absolutely nothing carnal in the way she was so innocently sleeping, except for the way the sheet was drifting lower, lower...

The morning light lingered on her body, the rose-tipped breasts that he'd touched and held, the slender curve of her hip...

Closing his eyes didn't help. Jason wanted to move, but wisely he told his feet to get a clue. One hand flexed, then the other, so Jason told his hands to grow a pair and deal. Sadly, his cock stayed where it was, miserable and alone. Deep in his heart, Jason knew he could control his feet and his hands, but his dick was being a dick, and knowing he couldn't stand there forever, Jason stalked toward the shower, a little louder than he normally would have because he wanted freaking Sleeping Beauty to wake up. He wanted Sleeping Beauty to throw back the covers, the sunrise following the curves and the shadows and...

Realizing the situation was deteriorating fast, Jason fled. Once in the shower, he set the water on ice-cube cold and waited for his hard-on to wither away. Nada. He counted to one hundred in base ten. He recited the first nineteen digits of pi and still nothing changed. With one hand braced against the tile wall, he designed a new water controller in his head. It didn't help.

Seventeen minutes later, his skin was blue, his fingers were prunes, but his brainless cock didn't care, and so for the tenth time in four days, he reached down and took himself in hand.

One-eyed Kincaid. Miserable, full-cocked, one-eyed Kincaid.

At this rate, his other eye would go blind, too.

WHILE JASON TURNED HIMSELF into an icicle, Brooke smiled to herself, letting the warm sun linger where he'd looked. Ah, it was bliss to see a man in such pain. To see his face so hard with lust. She liked it when he looked like that, so intense, so focused, so needy...for her.

It was too bad he was suffering alone in the shower, but that was the agreement, and that was what was smart, and frankly, he didn't deserve her until he admitted how much he needed a woman in his bed. Not just any woman, though. No, only her.

Still, it was a shame that he was so stubborn and wasn't there now. A crying shame, she thought, remembering the way his big body felt on top of her, feeling him push deep inside her, his hard chest rough against her breasts. In the warm sun, her nipples grew achy, and her hips arched, searching for him, wanting him. Desire flowed through her, as soft as the sun, and she could feel her body swell. From the other room, she could hear the sounds of his shower, knew the water was darkening his hair, glistening on his chest, running down his long legs...

Soon Brooke reached between her legs, imagining his hands there, his hungry mouth on her breasts. If she closed her eyes, it was his body covering her, his industrious finger pleasuring her, his burning touch that was heating her skin.

Faster she stroked, her eyes tightly closed, her hips straining to meet him. Finding nothing above her but cool air, her teeth cut into her lip, willing her hand to be longer, thicker, warmer...

But, no...

Furious with him, furious with her useless hand, Brooke swore and opened her eyes.

The Captain.

He was leaning against the doorjamb, a towel wrapped around his waist, not that it mattered because the man was huge when aroused. Brooke froze on the spot, legs splayed open, her body exposed.

If she smiled at him, if she opened her arms...

But, no. Instead she stared, melting under his white-hot gaze, willing him to take the step.

Only one.

It was humiliating to endure, her eyes pleading, her thighs wide, and the Captain standing fast. Eventually her eyes drifted closed.

For a long, long time there was only the lonely silence, and when Brooke dared to look again, the Captain was gone.

THEY DIDN'T SPEAK for most of the afternoon—thankfully. Every time Jason happened to glance in her direction, all he could picture was the heavy invitation in her eyes, the glistening dark curls between her legs, the swollen pink flesh that begged to be filled.

His cock would never recover. Ever.

His cock's opinion notwithstanding, he knew he'd done the right thing. Brooke was too vulnerable. When she got her own place, when she told her brother that she was basically broke and Hart told her he didn't care, then she'd be glad that Jason had been the sensible one.

He noticed as she bent over a milk crate, her shirt gaping open, the line between her breasts damp with sweat. He wished that he'd never tasted her, never taken her. Best to ignore her, best to forget.

It was while studiously ignoring her non-presence that he ripped his finger on a jagged piece of metal. He swore, not loud enough that she could hear, because if she wasn't concerned about him bleeding to death, he'd be happy to die in her ignorance of that fact.

However, Brooke didn't seem concerned, picking through a collection of old vacuum radio tubes. Mumbling something unpleasant, Jason escaped inside to bandage his thumb. As he passed by the kitchen, he spotted a strange object hanging over the sink. A piece of wire, twisted into two cirlces with four dangling wires. Yellow resistors had been threaded onto the wire, and from the top circle extended a red Zener diode. It was either a hippopotamus or a... Jason cracked a smile.

A unicorn.

A note was attached to the rear leg.

"In case you forgot, I'll be joining Austen and Gillian for dinner tonight. There is chicken salad in the

refrigerator. I will try and restrain myself from doing
anything embarrassing.
Your eternally loyal employee."

Jason laughed. It didn't matter how bad things were in
Brooke's world, it didn't register with her. A more level-
headed man might have called her delusional, the way she
plodded ahead, ignoring all the warning signs in front of
her. But there was something fascinating about her world
that made a less level-headed man want to stay and explore.
Listen to the pure joy of her laugh, see the happiness she
found in the ordinary, lick the sweat from the golden skin
of her breasts.

Hell.

Shaking off the lust, Jason reminded himself that *platonic* was the word of the day. And platonic did much to
explain why he spent the next two hours rigging up an
old computer terminal display. By mounting a wireless
router to it, he could send messages to the display via his
phone. Best of all, the portable motion sensor would alert
him when someone was skulking around. Elaborate, yes.
Overkill, probably. Egotistical, definitely.

And somebody was definitely curious. He could see her
spying on him as he lugged the computer into the house,
where he wedged it on the kitchen counter between the vise
and rotary saw. Three minimal modifications later and his
first message was glowing in eerie 1970s' green.

"Sarcasm is not pretty. Thank you for the chicken
salad. Is that dill or arsenic?
Your extraordinarily patient boss."

He stood back and admired his own genius, then returned outside. Brooke stood underneath the shade netting,

clipboard in hand, unmoved by his genius or pretending to be unmoved. However, it was a mere twenty minutes later that the motion sensor triggered the alarm on his phone. Not so unmoved after all, he thought, aware that she was no longer nearby.

Patiently he waited until she returned to the yard, then he pocketed the gasket he'd been meaning to attach to the faucet and went to investigate what she'd done. Inside he found a new note hanging from the unicorn.

"Since sarcasm is not pretty, I thought you would be more likely to appreciate it. Your bandage is turning red. Please make sure the bleeding stops. If you need assistance with a tourniquet, I'm very good at knots. Your medically talented employee."

Quickly he changed his bandage, and escaped to the privacy of one of his sheds before he texted his response.

"I am touched by your charity but, no, I don't need medical attention. There is a fifty on the table. We need milk. And you could buy shoes. See, that is how charity works.
Your even-tempered and generous boss."

Shortly after that, Brooke changed her clothes, skipping down the porch steps with a pink scarf tied around her neck. She had stolen some of his white light-emitting diodes, using them as a light-up hair ornament. Mutely she glided toward him, nodded once, and then he watched as she drove off in her wreck of a car. Exactly forty-seven minutes passed before he allowed himself to read her response.

"I took the fifty. You owe me for today's work. I don't
need shoes. My boots are awesome. Maybe I'll buy
a vibrator instead. Don't wait up.
Your self-sufficient employee."

Jason tilted his head back and laughed.

THE CAPTAIN WAS WAITING up for her when she got home,
and at first, she pretended as if she didn't see him sitting
in the kitchen, a half-gutted cylindrical gadget laying out
on the table. Not that it was really a kitchen with the piles
of tools, the clunky air compressor, and the neatly organized rows of milk crates along the wall. She liked that he
was at peace amongst the chaos. It never flustered him or
frustrated him. No, the Captain was a very passive man
for a soldier.

"How was dinner?" he asked casually.

"Good," she answered, equally causally, leisurely stroll-
ing across the room, clutching the brown paper bag to her
chest. It was empty, there was no vibrator, but he was intrigued yet trying not to look intrigued and Brooke mentally patted herself on the back.

The Captain inspected the bag, met her eyes and then
buried himself back in his task. Okay, not so successful
after all.

"How was your brother?"

"Good," she replied.

"Did you tell him?" he asked, still not looking at her.

Brooke stopped, aware of the knot in her stomach. It
wasn't a fun, sexual tension knot, but the less fun, truthi-
ness knot. "Tell him what?"

"Tell him where you're staying."

"No."

"Is he nice to you?"

She knew the words were an effort for him. The Captain wasn't a man for light conversation, but at least he was giving it a try. "I think he's warming. Given time, I'm sure we can establish a solid foundation, and at that point, I'll explain my situation."

At that, his scar silvered in the fluorescent lights. "Can I ask you a question?"

Another surprise.

"Are you sure you want to?"

"Yes."

She leaned against the sofa, the very place where he was going to sleep tonight—alone—and sniffed. All across America, men were sleeping on couches because their women had kicked them out of the bed. Trust the Captain to be the exception. "You should understand that asking questions implies something more than a traditional employer-employee relationship, and I'm not sure that it's covered in our agreement."

The Captain stayed silent, which told her much about his opinion of her snarky remark.

"I'm sorry." Charlene Hart had been snarky when she drank, and although Brooke knew she had picked up some of Charlene's less than admirable habits, that didn't mean she had to like it.

"It's about time somebody besides me gets to apologize."

"I try not to screw up," she told him, and she did. Lately, she seemed to be doing it less. Apparently his meticulous nature was starting to rub off on her, which was a good thing. Details had never been her strong point. "I think I'm doing a better job at not screwing up than you," she added, only because it wasn't very often she could feel superior. It felt nice to flaunt it.

"Can we get back to the question?"

"Talking about your mistakes is a lot more fun," she answered, neatly dodging the question.

"Brooke," he said, frustration in his voice.

"Captain," she answered, with a pointed glance at the tiny sofa, equally frustrated.

"What happened?"

As probing questions went, it was pretty much the worst. She didn't like the abnormalities in her life. She didn't like feeling like a freak, someone who never belonged anywhere, but out of all the people she'd ever met, it was the Captain who would probably understand best. She suspected he'd had his share of abnormalities as well, and he didn't seem to care. Brooke dropped the useless sack on the couch, her fingers locked on the hard back for support, and then took a long breath.

"My mother was a very nice woman with what she called a joyous spirit, which meant she loved her spirits a little too much—usually vodka because it doesn't smell. She had very little education and very few skills, and since she wasn't very fond of the drudgery of the workplace, she usually avoided working and would hook up with whatever kind stranger wanted to take her and her daughter in."

Just as she'd expected, he didn't look surprised or disapproving. No matter the way the wind blew, the Captain stood tall. "Where did the two of you live?"

"A lot of places. The road was our home."

"When did she die?"

"January 1, 2002. Cirrhosis of the liver, although there was no confirmed diagnosis. I just assumed."

"You've been alone since then?"

"Yes."

"Working?"

"Some. I lived in Rhode Island for some time, a receptionist for a chiropractor, Dr. Morgan Downey Knox, the third. He was very particular about the way I answered the phone, but I was able to improve my vocabulary. While I was working in the doctor's office, I looked up Tyler, and arranged the meeting in New York. My mother didn't like to talk about my brothers, or my father, or Texas, but I knew a little and I wanted to know more. I thought creating this great life in New York would convince them that I was normal, but it took a large pile of cash, pretty much everything I had."

"You are normal."

"No one's normal," she said, smiling at the one-eyed man surrounded by left-behind parts.

"There's a point. So why do you want to be normal?"

"Don't you?" she asked, but she knew the answer. She just wanted to understand why.

He shook his head, not giving her the answer she wanted. The Captain was a tricky man, particular about his secrets and not wanting people to know he was tricky. Being particular about her secrets as well, Brooke understood.

"Can I ask you a question?" she finally asked, because this was important.

The Captain considered it and then nodded. "Seems fair."

"Why do you do all this? Why all the repairing and the fixing and the creating?" As probing questions went, it was pretty much the worst, but she figured the tricky man owed her.

"Because nobody else does."

"You like to be different?"

"Different?" He frowned at her choice of words, scratched at the brown stubble of his jaw. "It's not different. It just is."

"What's the best thing you ever created?"

His uncovered eye narrowed, not so impassive, not so

comfortable now. He liked living in chaos, but the worst sort of chaos was the chaos inside. That sort of chaos wasn't so easy to fix. Brooke understood that, too.

"That's question number two."

"You can have a question number two if you'd like," she countered. It was only fair.

At first she didn't think he would answer, but eventually he did, because in the end, the Captain was a fair man, too.

"I was a maintenance officer in Iraq. The *muj's* were blowing up all sorts of shit, soldiers, too. Standard issue wasn't working for the trucks, so we had to get creative. They needed metal plating, shields to protect from the blast. So, me and Mad Max, we started scrounging whatever we could get our hands on, and we hobbled together some of the butt-ugliest transports ever. It worked. The *muj* still tried to blow up shit, but after that, men came home. Finally the beltway clerks pulled their head out and got wise to the problem, and then the Humvees rolled off fully loaded with one thousand pounds of ballistic-resistant American steel. But for a while, me and Max, we did some good work."

The Captain smiled at her then, and Brooke smiled back. Good work, indeed. Brave, resourceful, matter-of-fact. Most of the world would never know, which was too bad because the rest of the world could learn much from Jason Kincaid. "Why did you enlist?"

He shrugged. "Seemed like the right thing to do at the time."

"Why did you leave?"

"That's question number four," he reminded her.

"I'll give you four questions," she offered generously, because she liked this cautious give and take, and if he was willing, then Brooke believed she should be willing, too.

"I stopped being useful, and didn't want to sit behind a

desk." After he finished, he waited, watching her expectantly. Give and take.

"Your turn."

"After your mother died, why'd you stay on the road?"

Why? "Nowhere was home. I kept trying to find it."

"Is this home?" he asked, a deceptively simple question. This small town—where she'd never lived before—felt like more of a home than anywhere else, but it wasn't because of her brother, or the Hart land, or the chatty dinners at the Wanamaker house. If she told him the truth, would he put up one thousand pounds of ballistic-resistant American steel? She glanced down at the couch and smiled to herself. When she looked up, maybe there was more in her eyes than she wanted, but hopefully a man with fifty-percent vision would only see half as much. "It's a start. What about you? Is this home?"

His one good eye looked at her, looked through her, and Brooke's fingers gripped the cushions a little harder.

"I don't need a home."

"Everybody needs a home," she insisted. Everyone, including the Captain. Especially the Captain, who was normally a very intelligent man. But there were some things that the Captain pretended not to see, and she believed it was time someone pointed them out. Nicely, of course.

He shrugged again, brushing off her words. She longed to shake him, wake him up to the world, but the Captain was a tricky man, surrounding himself with Dog, the tools, the half-gutted cylindrical doo-hickey...

Then Brooke began to feel whole, a little wiser. He'd made a home, he just never knew it. With that, she walked over, kissed him once on the cheek, a silent invitation in her eyes, not so hidden this time. However, the Captain was a hard man who believed that the world didn't need him, and he stared impassively.

Completely unfooled, Brooke retrieved her empty paper bag from the couch. The empty paper bag containing her imaginary vibrator, which she fondled as if it were a man. The Captain turned pale. "Knock, next time," she instructed, and then strolled away, satisfied with his quiet moan. Wisely, she hid her grin.

TWO DAYS LATER, when Brooke awoke, she pulled her money from her boot, counted it out and beamed. More than enough for shoes. The Captain was already outside, taking apart some large metal tank, and Brooke approached with a spring in her step, because finally...finally, the world's ugliest boots were going into the trash.

"I need to go to town."

He pulled off his cap, put down the drill in his hand. "Shoes?"

She didn't care for his judgmental assumption, even if it was the truth. Her right boot had a hole on top, and the West Texas dust had turned both shoes an unfashionable pasty gray. "Possibly. If I'm so inclined."

Then he smiled at her and she decided she didn't mind his assumption quite so much. "Good. Tallyrand's has the best selection. Or, if you want, we can drive into Austin. There's a great scrap yard on the east side of town."

Normally she would have agreed, but when funds were limited, shopping was a blood sport best done alone. "Tallyrand's will be fine. Maybe Rita will have time for a chat."

"Rita always has time for a chat." He paused, tugged at the bill of his cap. "What are you going to tell her?"

"Does it matter?"

"I should know, in case anyone asks."

"You're my boss. That's the truth."

He nodded. "The truth is always the easiest. No open toes."

"Excuse me?"

He pointed at her feet. "No sandals."

"Does this workplace now have a dress code?"

"Do you want to rip your toe off?"

Well, when he put it like that. "No. However, in defer-
ence to your somewhat overwrought, safety-first attitude,
I'll find something practical, yet still cute."

He smiled again, a quicksilver tilt to his mouth. "Good
luck with that."

Boldly, because Brooke was never safety-first, she rose
up and pressed a kiss to that quicksilver mouth. Automati-
cally he pressed back, and for a few precious seconds, they
were joined. Before he could move away, she stepped back
and was rewarded with a quick flash of disappointment in
his eye. Then the normally passive gray gaze returned and
"Humph" was all he said before picking up his drill.

It was a good thing he couldn't see her grin.

THE TOWN OF TIN CUP came alive early on weekdays, the
streets full of pickup trucks, delivery trucks, shopkeepers
opening their stores. Yes, everyone was opening except Mr.
Hadley's law offices. Apparently, Mr. Cervantes wasn't as
diligent as she had hoped. Brooke shoved a note through
the mail slot in the door, and then dropped in to Hinkle's
grocery to restore some of the long-lost Hart honor. Gladys,
still remembering the shoplifted can of peas, treated Brooke
suspiciously until Brooke complained about the weather,
just like she'd seen Gillian do. Weather complaints seemed
to be the quickest way to mend fences, and then Gladys
complained about her gall stones, and by the time Brooke
left the store, she knew she'd won the older woman over.

Down the street, Tallyrand's was full, farmers picking
up their weekly feed supplies. The line was curled halfway around the store, and one barrel-jawed old man wasn't

Send For
2 FREE BOOKS
Today!

I accept your offer!

Please send me two
free Harlequin® Blaze®
novels and two mystery
gifts (gifts worth about $10).
I understand that these books
are completely free—even the
shipping and handling will be
paid—and I am under no obligation
to purchase anything, ever, as explained
on the back of this card.

151/351 HDL FEHC

Please Print

FIRST NAME

LAST NAME

ADDRESS

APT.#   CITY

STATE/PROV.   ZIP/POSTAL CODE

Visit us online at
www.ReaderService.com

happy, complaining in a loud voice. Rita ignored him, and the old man's voice grew louder before Brooke stepped in, asking about the weather, asking about his crops, until finally the old man lightened up, blushing under all the attention. Rita noticed, just as Brooke had hoped, and shot her a grateful smile.

A person could never collect too many friends. Having friends was the first step to belonging.

Once the line was cleared, Brooke found the shoes and now Rita was definitely ready to chat. Today, the former beauty queen was dressed in tight-fitting jeans tucked into ornate boots, and a burnt orange and white glitter vest.

"How long have you known the Captain?" Rita asked.

"Two weeks. When I first arrived in town, I was searching for a job. He needed help, and I applied."

"I didn't know the Captain was hiring."

"Oh, yes. He stays very busy."

"Doing what?" Rita pretended to dust off her glass display shelves, but Brooke wasn't fooled. This conversation would be relayed in its entirety to pretty much anybody as soon as Brooke was out the door. No, Rita was an excellent way to upgrade the Captain's reputation in the community.

"The Captain fixes things. He owns a thriving repair business."

"Business? He doesn't take any money for that. The widow Kenley called him about her broken washing machine that up and died, and he told her not to worry about it. He'd take care of everything."

"And he does a little art work on the side," Brooke told her, not wanting Rita to think that the Captain was some mere Maytag repairman.

"Art?" Rita raised a beautifully penciled brow. "The Captain? He's an artist?"

After glancing around, pretending to check for lurking

ears, Brooke motioned for Rita to move closer and spoke in a hushed whisper. "He's a very talented artist. You should see some of the things that he's done."

"Paintings?" Rita whispered back.

Brooke picked up a set of cowbell windchimes and listened to the hollow clanging sound, deciding that cowbells were not the best choice in making windchimes.

Next to the wind chimes was a shelf full of cactus, the prickly pear kind, guaranteed to thrive in all climates or your money back, at least that was what the sign claimed. Brooke picked up the small plant, tested the sharp prickles and promptly put it back.

"Not paintings exactly," Brooke explained. "I think his stuff defies the structure of most artistic genres, but you know how the art world is. Always wanting to put things into a box. When you stare into the soul of one of the Captain's pieces, it's like techno-art crossed with steampunk crossed with a very efficient environmental message. I simply call it 'the Kincaid.'"

"Really? I had no idea. I never could figure out why he would want to move to Tin Cup after he left the service. Didn't know anybody but Sonya's aunt and uncle, Gladys and Henry, and they weren't that close. We always thought he was traumatized by the war. PTSD."

"Oh, no. He's very, very normal. Eccentric, but normal."

"You seem to know him very well."

"I understand his work."

"Do you have an art background?"

If one counted the year's worth of auction house catalogs she'd picked up in New York, then sure. "I dabble."

"How's your brother?"

"I had dinner with him and his fiancée last night, as a matter of fact. Love the ring."

At that, Rita frowned. "You saw it?"

"Well, yes, she's not very shy about it. But it's sweet, seeing them together. He seems to have done a lot of really great things for the town."

"I know, I know. He seems to have gotten his act together, sure, but we all know he's got some no-good mischief in his past, and those memories don't get washed away so easily."

This was the second time that people were accusing the Hart family of criminal acts. However, Brooke liked Rita, she wanted a discount on the smart pair of leather ankle boots that were sitting on the side table, and she wasn't going to argue. "It seems like he's really turned things around."

"It's the Sheriff's doing."

"Maybe Austen had something to do with it, as well," Brooke added, needing to defend her brother in some way. "The Hart family is very civic-minded."

"I suppose."

"Can we talk about some shoes? There's one pair here, but there's a scratch on the leather."

Rita picked up the shoe, bright red lips pursed until they disappeared. "I have another pair somewhere. Let me get them for you."

Brooke pulled the woman back. "You know, I like these. I like the scratch, and I like you, Rita. Let me take these off your hands. Say, twenty-five percent off. I think that's fair for damaged merchandise."

"They're very good shoes, and twenty-five percent… Well, Brooke, honey, I'm just a struggling storeowner, and in these lean times…"

Right then the shop-bell rang, and a well-to-do lady came through the door. With perfect timing, Brooke held the shoe out in front of her, just as the new customer passed.

"It's a very large scratch. Almost a hole. And who wants a pair of shoes that already have a hole."

"There's no hole," Rita insisted, finally starting to look nervous.

Brooke smiled nicely. "Let me ask the lady what she thinks. I bet she thinks there's a hole."

Now genuinely alarmed, Rita grabbed the shoes, and pitched her voice low. "I'll go twenty-five," she said, wising up to the fact that Brooke was no amateur shopper.

Brooke nodded, followed her to the register, noticed the handmade sale signs and then felt a pang of conscience. Rita wasn't some billionaire shopkeeper rolling in the dough. This was her community, her family, and the Harts were supposed to be very civic-minded. "What you said earlier...if it's a problem, I could do twenty."

Rita gaped for a second, and then started to chuckle, as if surprised that generous thoughtfulness might come from a customer...or maybe it was only the Harts. "You're a cool customer, Brooke Hart, but I like you. For that, I'll go twenty percent and not a percentage point more."

"And the cactus, but I'll pay full price for that," Brooke told her, picking up one of the small plants, being careful not to get stuck. The Captain could use a few more living things around the house, and Brooke thought a cactus was the living thing most likely to survive under his care.

Satisfied with their agreement, Brooke counted out her cash and then took a quick peek at the new pair of shoes in her bag. Practical and still cute. The Captain should never have doubted her.

WHEN BROOKE CAME HOME, the first thing she did was to show off her purchase.

The Captain watched and made primordial *humph*

sounds as she twisted her foot one way, then the other. "You could have found something more solid."

"They're leather. The soles are some specially designed long-lasting rubber. And they look great with jeans."

He made another *humph* sound, took another look at her shoes, took a long look at Brooke and then walked away.

This time, it was Brooke who made the primordial *humph* sound. This hands-off, safety-first attitude was getting old. She had forgiven him his earlier missteps, mainly because he was too nice of a man for her to be angry with. The Captain cared. She'd been careful not to be too slutty this time, better to ease him back into her bed. Thinking strategically wasn't something that came naturally to her. Charlene Hart didn't have a strategic bone in her body, and she'd been the sole role model in Brooke's life, so Brooke didn't fault herself for not having developed that quality yet, but she noticed that the Captain was very strategic. He could spend long minutes staring at an engine or part, prodding it gently, turning it over in his hands like a clump of clay. Everything the Captain did involved forethought and planning and patience.

Later that afternoon, she investigated the far side of the house, where a line of tarp-covered piles dotted the ground like tents. Under the first tarp, she discovered a treasure trove of old sinks, basins, faucets and one extralarge claw-foot tub. It was a beauty, with generous sides and an elegantly sloped back that rose higher than the front. Down the side of each leg was a raised design of some sort, and kneeling on the ground, she wiped at the grime, delighted to discover that it was a dainty mix of hearts and lilies entwined.

"You want to put something in that? It's a little heavy to haul things in, but I could put some wheels on it..." the Captain said, coming to stand beside her.

"It's perfect," she announced, picturing how it would look, gleaming white, overflowing with bubbles. Completely impractical and yet...

"Not without wheels. How do you move it?"

"It's not a container, it's a bathtub." For once, amid all the mechanical doodads and gizmos, little Brooke Hart could educate the Captain.

"Yes, I can see that," he answered, completely deflating her mood.

"You don't move bathtubs. You put them in one place, run water into them, and then bathe."

It was rather fascinating to watch the Captain experience a lightbulb moment. His forehead furrowed as the wheels turned, and then when everything clicked into place, his head tilted slightly to the left, and then he would nod once, mainly to himself, as if the universe was aligned again. "Do you want a bathtub?" he asked, and Brooke giggled.

"It was a serious question," he added, looking a little hurt.

"It won't fit in my car," Brooke explained, wondering why he hadn't grasped the impracticality of the situation.

"What about here? My place."

Her heart missed a beat.

"Here?" she probed carefully, aware of the many subtleties in the one small word, but of course, the Captain wouldn't be aware of such nuances in his question.

"Here. For now. At some point in time, you'll have a place of your own, but for now...here."

And then she realized he was serious and she was surprised at how much the idea hurt. Not the owning a bathtub part, but the idea of leaving one behind. Brooke had a lot of experience in leaving things behind. Usually it didn't hurt, but that was probably because she'd never had anything worth keeping before.

Brooke rose to her feet, and wiped her palms on her jeans. "That's too much trouble. And it wouldn't fit in the bathroom. Besides, I love showers. Much more efficient, and quick. Who knows when the hot water's going to go. No, showers are a lot smarter."

"Haven't had a lot of bathtubs, have you?"

"Some," she admitted. Fourteen was the exact number, not that anyone was counting.

"I could…" he started.

She held up her hand before he did something that made it even harder for her to leave. "No."

His mouth tightened, but he didn't argue.

"I'll use it to put the do-me-hootchers in," she rambled on. "I was looking for something extra-large."

"Do-me-hootchers?"

"Those," she explained, picking up a small, elongated… do-me-hootcher.

The Captain met her eyes, but Brooke was a little smarter now and kept her own eyes carefully blank. "Those are Geiger counters from the second world war."

"Geiger counters," she repeated, storing it away in her head. "Then the tub will fit the bill nicely."

"I'll put the wheels on it tomorrow," he promised.

THE NEXT MORNING, the bathtub disappeared and she told herself it didn't matter. Someday when she had a fine bathroom, she would buy a heart-stopping tub. Something big, modern, with jets because who needed old fashioned frills? Completely impractical, and until then, showers were great. They were hearty and invigorating and…

Once more she glanced toward the empty spot and sighed. It had been pretty, with the curly-cue legs and the back designed to ease well-worn muscles. *Oh, well. Things to do, abandoned gadgets to sort.*

To keep herself busy, she took the tiny cactus and placed it on the window-sill in the kitchen, right next to some sort of meter. What the meter measured, she didn't know, but it set off her cactus nicely. After cleaning the dust from her hands, she went back outside, wondering how long it would take the Captain to notice the plant.

Not like she was noticing him. Earlier he had abandoned his work shirt for a cooler tank top, and sweat poured lovingly down his back. Every time he lifted a heavy tool, the sturdy muscles in his arms bunched. He had a steady, powerful rhythm, pulverizing the hapless metal into a quivering mass of pliable goo. Her mouth felt dry and her thighs began to quiver, and she put a hand on the porch railing for support.

Yes, there were lots of things to do, the Captain among them, but she was learning to be patient, as well.

IT TOOK TWO DAYS FOR Brooke to make the perfect batch of brownies. The first night, the Captain had watched her silently. The next night, he abandoned his latest project and offered to help.

"You know how to make brownies?" she asked, curious because up to this point, the Captain had demonstrated no culinary abilities at all.

"I can follow instructions," he said, coming to stand next to her, peering over her shoulder into the bowl.

"So can I," she told him, in case he thought she needed assistance.

"I should learn," he admitted, and grudgingly, too. It made her happy to know this wasn't about lack of faith in her abilities, but a lack of faith in his own.

"How to make brownies? They're very easy," Brooke told him, efficiently cracking two eggs in the bowl, dropping in one small shell in the process. Quickly she fished it out with her finger. "You're supposed to use a spoon, but sometimes I cheat—to make sure it tastes okay."

Brooke licked at her finger, noticed the Captain watching and made a long production of taste-testing, curious to see exactly how much self-control the Captain acutally had.

His gray eyes darkened to black, and she could feel his growing erection brushing against her thigh. Her pulse quickened and, deciding on bold action, she offered up her chocolate-covered finger.

The Captain took a cautious step back. "I should learn to do more in the kitchen."

Patience and strategy, she reminded herself.

"Did Sonya do all the cooking?" Brooke asked, not sure he would answer, but tonight, to her surprise, he did.

"I was away most of the time."

"What about your mother?"

"Mom always cooked. Great stuff—meat loaf, crab cakes. She made a Thanksgiving turkey that would knock your socks off."

"You miss her?"

A shadow of loneliness crossed her face, and she felt the ache cut through her heart. "Yeah."

"What about the rest of your family?"

At her question the loneliness was gone, as if it never existed. "I thought you wanted to make brownies."

"Families are important," she told him, because loneliness could be hidden, but it never disappeared. This she knew well.

The Captain laughed. "Says the woman who's dodging her brother until she reaches some arbitrary number in her bank account."

"The brownies are for Austen. I'm going to see him tomorrow."

"Good," he said, and his hand reached out, touched her mouth. Brooke forgot to breathe.

Gently he brushed at her mouth, her cheek, and the ache in his eyes made her dizzy. "Chocolate."

"Of...course," she said, stumbling over the simple words.

His touch disappered, her breathing resumed and the intimate moment was gone, as if it never existed. Brooke poured in the last of the flour, still warm from his touch, because tenderness could be hidden but it never disappeared, either. The Captain possessed more tenderness than he knew.

Carefully she added the salt and baking powder, measuring each amount precisely. The Captain's close presence made precision difficult, but she thought she managed beautifully.

"You're going to see him, talk to him, show him what a great person you are? Or are you going to make something else up?"

The confident way he said it made her want to believe him. Made her want to think that Austen would welcome her as a sister. But the few times she'd seen her brother, welcoming wasn't even close.

She beat at the better until her hand began to hurt. Without a word, the Captain took over. "I'm bringing brownies," she told him, stilling his hand when the mixture was glossy and rich.

"You don't need the brownies, Brooke. He'll like you. I swear."

She saw the faith in his one good eye and it made her want to believe, but a lifetime of disappointment was hard to shake. Once the brownies were in the oven, she smiled at him and dusted the flour from her hands. "A little insurance never hurt."

THERE WAS SOMETHING very satisfying about tearing into a wall with a sledge hammer. The plaster kicked up a god-awful amount of dust, but Austen coughed happily, watching the destruction of his old home. He'd never felt right about putting a new house over the old one, however, this piece of the land would make a kick-ass garage where he could work on the Mustang. Or maybe he could find a sweet GT-40 for Gillian. He pulled back the hammer, ready to do some more damage when he saw the twin beams cutting through the dark.

There were headlights flickering up the drive. Not Gillian's high-powered halogens. These were different. Older.

Impala older.

Instantly, he knew. It was Brooke. His sister.

Austen tossed down the hammer, wiped the dust from his face and conjured up a smile that was worthy of greeting long-lost relatives. Even the ones that made your stomach tighten in knots.

As she picked her way through the debris, Austen shook his head apologetically. "I wasn't going to stay out her very long. Gillian's expecting me at the house for dinner, and I try to keep her happy."

"I could help you," she offered, looking so eager that he almost agreed.

"Nah. I've got it covered," he said. She seemed disappointed, and he reminded himself to be nicer to her.

"I can't stay very long anyway. I just wanted to give you these," she said, holding out a plate of brownies. Brownies. His sister had made him brownies.

"Wow. That's really nice and all. Are they homemade?"

"They are."

Austen stared at the paper plate, and the plastic-wrap covering, and realized what was wrong with this picture. "Brownies. How'd you make brownies at the Inn?" As soon

as he saw the horror in her eyes, he wanted to kick himself
for saying the wrong thing. Of course they weren't homemade, but she'd gone out of her way to make them look
homemade and now he'd gone and embarrassed her.

However, to her credit, she recovered quickly. "I borrowed the kitchen."

"You went to a lot of trouble for me. Thank you."

"You're my brother. I don't mind."

There was a long silence, and Austen winced, trying
to think up casual conversation. Making casual conversation was a necessary requirement in the field of politics,
but somehow, with Brooke, his mind always went blank.
Desperate, he blurted out the first thing that popped into
his head. "How are you getting along in town? People treat-
ing you okay?"

"Everyone has been very nice," she told him, sounding
as if she meant it.

"Wasn't expecting that, but miracles happen all the
time."

The silence dragged on, and he could see some of the
light fading from her eyes. "I should go," she said, and
began to walk away. Like a jerk, he nearly let her.

"Brooke!"

"Yeah?"

"Have you talked to Hadley?"

"No. He hasn't called. I left a message with Mr. Cervantes and put a couple of notes in the door, but nothing
yet."

"I don't know the number at Hadley's father's place, but
Gillian could get it. I could call."

"There's no rush," she said. "I've liked staying here and
wandering aorund the town. Seeing where you all lived.
What was it like living here?"

At first, he thought about lying. Making up some story

that would fit her fairy-tale theory, but this time, when he looked at her, he noticed soething different. A sturdiness and a strength. And she was his sister, after all.

"We didn't have a good time of it. Frank was mean. See that tree?" Austen pointed to the oak in the front yard. "Those holes? Frank like to take his Winchester and shoot at the tree. Stupidest thing you ever saw, but that was our father, Frank Hart. Drunk and stupid. Sometimes I would make up conversations with Mom. Have these long talks wither her in my head."

It was hard to keep the bitterness out of his voice, and unfortunately, Brooke had noticed.

"I should go," she said, and he watched her leave, holding the plate of brownies like a fool.

"Listen, these are great," he called after her. "We'll do dinner again, real soon."

WHEN BROOKE RETURNED HOME, the Captain was waiting on the porch. He'd hauled up a red leather bench seat and was sitting on it, like a swing.

"How'd it go?" he asked, and she sat down beside him, running a hand over the glossy material. It was one more overlooked item that the Captain had restored, making it shiny and useful again.

"He liked the brownies."

"You okay?"

"Yeah." She traced the lines of the seat, not really wanting to talk about Austen. If she had made great progess, if she had restored their relationship to something shiny and useful, maybe she would have felt better. "I like this. What's it from?"

"Nineteen sixty-seven Cadillac DeVille."

She didn't say much, and the Captain must have known

something was wrong. He reached out and took her hand and stayed with her, watching the night.

It was so peaceful here. The dark sky stretched beyond forever, but she didn't feel alone. The Captain was the quietest man she'd ever met, the hard security of his hand invited her to confide. "It's not a quick process, is it? Getting someone to like you."

"I don't think you'll have too many problems. You're easy to like."

"Thank you. You are, too."

"You're not very picky. You like everybody."

"Almost everybody," she corrected. "But I still don't have a lot of friends."

"I don't, either. I've learned not to lose sleep over it."

Off in the distance, she could see the lights of town, a cheery beacon in the night, but she wouldn't have traded anything for this.

"What happened with Max?"

"What do you mean?"

"The status is still in the box, and you don't forget. So I'm assuming there's a reason you haven't mailed it."

Next to her, she could feel the tension run through him and she realized her mistake. "I didn't mean to pry. I'm sorry. You've been very good about not prying."

He didn't say anything for a long time, but then he kicked his boots out in front of him and leaned his head against the seat's back. A very relaxed pose, certainly, but the tension still hummed through him like a live wire.

"IED in Afghanistan. The medics got him halfway to Landstuhl before he died. It was last year. Christmas."

Oh. She wanted to comfort him, but she knew she was many months too late. Instead she squeezed his hand, wishing she could absorb all the tension inside him. All the tears that he would ever shed. "I'm sorry."

"Everybody dies."

He said it so easily, as if he had no feelings, as if he were as lifeless as the machines that he worked on. "Yes, and if you care, it always hurts," Brooke said softly.

He turned and stared at her, eyes as dark and mysterious as the night. "Did you hurt when your mother died?"

"Yes. I still loved her, even with the way she was. She was my mother. But I was more afraid than anything. She was all I had."

With his free hand, he reached out and stroked her hair, one touch, before his hand fell away. "I wish I'd been there."

"I wish I'd been here when Max died."

"Me, too."

There were so close, so perfectly aligned, and Brooke felt the stutter in her heart. "Captain?"

Abruptly, he stood. "I'm going inside. You should get some sleep."

After he left her, she stayed a few moments, watching the orange moon burn high on the horizon. But soon, the air blew cooler, the dark felt gloomier and the magic of the night had gone.

THE NEXT WEEK PASSED slowly, with the Captain maintaining a determinedly distant presence.

Brooke had little experience with seduction. The few times in her past that she'd actually desired sex with a man, they had been more than willing, and after she'd taken her pleasure, she had sent them on their way. No muss, no fuss. All was simple and straightforward, with little effort at all, but not with the Captain. No, he had ignored her subtle invitations and long come-hither glances. By the time Wednesday had rolled around, Brooke decided to abandon attempts at nuance. Previously, the obvious had worked successfully, so tonight the obvious seemed the way to go again.

After dinner was over, when the Captain had assumed his customary place, turning the kitchen table into a work table, Brooke seized the opportunity to unbutton her shirt. Three buttons were free before he noticed.

His gaze was locked on her hands, the tic was back in his jaw, and the screwdriver was digging into the table's surface, but she didn't think he realized all that. "What are you doing?" he asked. A silly question.

"I'm getting comfortable. You're so busy I didn't think you would mind." Her fingers parted the shirt, pulled it off her shoulders, leaving her best sheer bra underneath. "Does this bother you?" she asked, an innocent smile on her face.

"Brooke."

She liked the way he said her name, low and graveled. The rough sound rolled down her spine and she shivered, not cold at all. Still smiling, she unbuttoned the fly on her jeans. "Is there a problem?"

"Yes."

Deciding there was no point in revisiting the argument, she pulled at the zip, easing the denim over her hips, enjoying the raw pain on his face. There was so little he ever exposed, hiding behind his patch and his scar.

Tonight, the gloves came off.

As would her bra.

Defiantly she unhooked the front clasp. "Ignore me. No problem." The clasp came loose. The Captain swallowed.

After easing the bra from her shoulders, Brooke dangled it over the couch.

The Captain didn't move.

If she had known he was going to be this difficult, she would have dressed in more layers. However, Brooke was accustomed to making do with the resources at hand, and she slid her thumbs in the wispy material of her panties, easing them down her legs.

The Captain still didn't move.

Undeterred, she sat on the couch, kicked her feet out on the coffee table in front of her, and turned the television on. Two could play the ignorant game.

It actually felt rather liberating, sitting in the nude, feeling his tortured gaze on her, and doing nothing at all. She leaned back, letting the warm night air drift over her, electric current dancing on her skin, her nipples peaked with the thrill.

The Captain stood and she held her breath, waiting. Slowly he approached, casting a glowering shadow over the couch, and she could feel every inch where he stared. She raised her head, met his eyes and felt her heart twist at the pain in his uninjured eye.

"Why are you doing this?"

Didn't he get it? "You are the best man I've ever known."

Patiently she waited for his response, because he would be the one. This time, he couldn't hide.

"That's not a good reason for sex."

Well, no, it spoke to things a lot more powerful than sex, but okay, if that's the way they were going to play it, then she was more than prepared to list all the good reasons for sex. "I watch you during the day, and I want to pull off your shirt and run my hands over your shoulders, feeling them tense where I touch. You have such strong, capable shoulders. Sometimes in my mind, I lay my head there, and I feel revived. I remember your mouth on my breasts, hard and hungry, and my nipples ache to be tasted again. And then I remember how you felt between my legs, filling me, loving me. I get so wet and lonely and I hurt. I don't want to hurt anymore. When I'm with you, when you hold me...I'm home."

There it was, the last of her secrets, and she had nothing else to give. She longed to look away, but she didn't. No, there wouldn't be two cowards in the room. His fingers gripped the edge of the couch, inching closer to her, but not close enough. "This isn't your home. I can never be what you want."

His words were designed to hurt her, she knew that, but it was *his* knuckles that were white against the brown cushions, not hers. Desire strained on his face, not hers. Quietly she rose, coming to stand in front of him, so close, but not close enough. "Stop fighting me, Captain. Stop fighting this." She kept her voice low and gentle. "Was it so bad with me?"

"No."

"Do you remember? Do you lay awake, feeling my mouth on you, my skin under your hands?"

The Captain nodded once, but made no move to touch her.

"Kiss me," she urged, praying for him to move.

He stared at her lips. "I love your mouth. So soft, so generous, so open."

Her lips parted at the pretty words, but in the end, they were only words. "Take it. Take me."

"I won't stop. I can't." His voice was harsh, not nearly so pretty this time.

"I know," she said, moving a whisper closer. All he had to do was reach out...

His fingers lifted to her hair, stroked the long length, traveling down her shoulder, resting possessively on the rise of her breast. One rough thumb rolled her nipple almost absently. Each stolen touch brought an answering pull between her legs, but this time Brooke stayed still, watching the heat in his eyes, the tightness to his mouth. "They're perfect. Like something in a dream."

The easy glide of his movements were hypnotizing, seductive, and she sighed as he explored her, memorized her. Gently he traced the curve of her hip, his hands calloused, but, oh, so careful. Those same hard hands moved behind her, cupping her cheeks, sliding lower, slipping lower.

Brooke's eyes flickered close, heavy with pleasure when he parted her thighs. Such marvelously efficient hands. A Captain's hands.

His fingers stroked her back and forth, and she could hear the rasp of his breathing, feel her body swell with desire. "So soft, so generous, so wet."

It was like something in a dream. A warm, liquid dream. When his fingers slipped inside her, Brooke's knees dipped, but the Captain was quick, and strong arms lifted her, laying her on the couch. Breathlessly she waited for him to cover her, but he knelt beside her, his hand returning between her thighs, and then the dream was back.

The steady touch of his fingers was like a melody, pleasure lapping over her. So easy, so quiet, so soft. Brooke gave herself over to him, her body rising and falling in time with his hand.

Then the melody disappeared and a moan of protest escaped from her mouth, but then she felt his mouth on her aching flesh. The quiet waves of pleasure disappeared, turning dark, dangerous.

His mouth was not nearly as safe as his hand, sucking on her flesh, pulling hard and insistent, and the exquisite pressure was too much. Her hands fisted into the cushion, pulling the material, helplessly fighting against it. She wanted the dream, the safe, gentle dream.

"Do you want me to stop?" he asked, and she knew what he was doing. Testing her, thinking that she would walk away. Brooke opened her heavy eyes, and glared. "No."

His smile was hard, and once again he lowered his head.

At first, she was prepared for the pressure, her body riding the waves, and she smiled to herself, but then his mouth found her sensitive nub, the friction of his tongue making her mutter, then swear, then finally scream. Colors flooded her mind, a frenzied kaleidoscope spinning faster and faster until she felt the world tremble around her.

The pressure disappeared, and her heart started to beat again. "Do you want me to stop?" he asked, his voice hard, his breathing ragged.

Her body felt limp, her eyes were too heavy to open, but the spirit would not be denied. *Did he really believe she was that weak?* Brooke waved a "continue" hand.

Then his finger pushed inside her, opening her, killing her, and then his hungry mouth moved again until it was more than she could take. She could feel the orgasm growing, mounting, before the orgasm crashed over her, ripping her in pieces. Her mouth opened to scream, to breathe, to damn the man to hell, but he was too quick, his mouth covering hers, his body blanketing hers. This time his tongue swept into her mouth, so gentle, so easy, but she wasn't fooled. Not this time.

Brooke tore at his shirt, declared war on his jeans until at last she could touch him, torture him as he had done her. Her fingers stroked his shaft, and she watched the pleasure flare in his eyes.

"I like the feel of you in my hands," she whispered to him.

"It's just a dick," he told her, inhaling sharply when she rolled the condom over his velvet skin.

"Not just," she answered, eyeing the part in question with respectful consideration.

When she looked up again, he was watching her, waiting, and in answer, she tilted her hips, feeling the head of his shaft against her.

"Take me, Captain. Please."

8

8

IT WAS THE ANSWER Jason needed, and he pushed inside her, feeling the give, feeling her stretch to accommodate him. Dark desirous eyes widened, locked on his face, her mouth open and wet. Quickly he covered her open mouth, blocked out her gaze, inching in farther, letting her slick heat block out everything but this.

Her body shifted to accommodate him, and with one powerful shove on his ass, Brooke embedded his thankless cock inside her.

His breathing stopped. His body frozen until he felt the soft stroke of her tongue in his mouth, across his lips. Then she opened drowsy eyes, the open-hearted gaze inspecting his face, his patch, his scar. At long last, she whispered, "Take me, Captain."

God help him, he did. Over and over he used her, trying to remember her pleasure, too, but she made him forget. So many things she made him forget.

Her generous mouth kissed his lips, the roughened skin of his scar and the marked blade of his shoulder. Her selfless fingers were never still, gliding over him like he was some damned sculpture. Brooke Hart was a foolish, foolish woman giving herself to him on the couch, on the floor.

Each time his gut would cramp up in guilt, she would flutter her lashes, expecting him to fall for her cheap tricks again—as if he could be easily conned. And then she would press her perfect breasts against him, not shy at all, until his simple-minded hands reached for her, and then no surprise there—his cock was rooting between her legs, wanting her once more.

By the time the sun was yawning outside, they'd made it to the bed, and she rose over him, flaunting that Hollywood body, murmuring with her pillow-top mouth, staring at him with adoring eyes that could make a man change his mind.

No, that Brooke Hart was trouble, he thought, letting her seduce him all over again.

THE PHONE RANG at precisely 9:17 a.m. Brooke was still in bed, rolled up in blankets and pillows, but Jason hadn't slept at all. He took the call outside the bedroom, keeping his voice low.

"Kincaid."

"I'm looking for Brooke Hart. She left this number. This is Hiram Hadley from the law offices of Harris and Howell."

The lawyer. Thoughtless jerk calling so early, he thought, glancing toward the bedroom. At the moment, Brooke was suffering from a serious lack of sleep, all due to Jason's conscienceless cock, and it didn't seem right to wake her. "She's not available now, but I know she's expecting your call. Could I get your number and I'll have her get back to you?"

Hadley sighed into the phone and if Jason had been a more accommodating man, he would have taken the hint and rolled Brooke out of bed. Not in this lifetime. "I'm still in North Dakota," Hadley said, "and don't have access to my papers, but I'm returning to Tin Cup next Wednesday and I can set up a meeting with her then. Do you know if she has a birth certificate?"

The suspicious tone wasn't winning the lawyer any friends, not that Jason had ever been fond of lawyers. Birth certificate? "I don't have a clue. Why don't you look it up?"

"There's no record of a Brooke Hart being born in Texas," the man explained patiently.

Jason didn't care. "I don't think she was born here. I bet you're going to have to check all the other states."

The lawyer sighed again, even louder. The old geezer was probably unhappy with the idea of extra work. Yeah, sometimes life sucked that way. "Do you know where Miss Hart was born?" he asked.

"Not a clue," Jason answered cheerfully.

"You'll tell her I'll be in on Wednesday? And if she could provide her birth cert—"

Jason hung up.

HE HAD FOUR OPPORTUNITIES to tell her, five if he counted lunch, but oddly enough, the words never came. Jason kept telling himself that since Hadley wasn't going to be around until the following week, what did it matter? It's not like Brooke could call him, instantly receive one-third of the Hart property—which wasn't worth squat—and then her life would be magically transformed.

Except for the mineral rights...

No, that was the kicker, the fly in the ointment, the shrapnel in the eye, because Jason Kincaid also knew there was an 86.3 percent probability of oil underneath the Hart land, mainly because there was a 100 percent probability of oil under his land. He'd known since they had finished running the tests last year. The suit that had delivered the results had eyed the acreage to the west—Hart land—and then explained in full, glorious detail how the formations below the surface worked.

Of course, Jason probably should have told his ex-wife, although legally Sonya didn't have any claim to it. At the time she'd been happily married to Tom, and money muddled people's vision. It dressed things up, made the previously unsightly sightly. Attractive. Appealing.

All smoke and mirrors, designed to cover the truth.

Usually a big fan of the truth, Jason was also a firm believer in the status quo, which was the probable reason that he didn't say a word to Brooke. To give himself credit, he didn't cop a feel when she asked him what a planer was. In fact, he was purposefully cool because last night had been a world-class lapse in judgment, especially since she'd be leaving him right after she talked to the lawyer. His conscience didn't ease up, especially watching her try to haul a lead water pump across the yard. Jason shook his head, picked up the thing himself, and lined it up with eight other pumps that he would most likely never use.

"Thank you, but I could have done it myself."

Then she blinked up at him, big, trusting eyes, and it was the perfect time to tell her about Hadley's call, but she was wearing a blue diode in her hair, and the freckles were starting to pop on her skin, and Jason's brain shut down. Before he knew it, the perfect time was gone.

AFTER EXTENDED HOURS of sexual congress, Brooke expected a little more intimacy from the Captain today. A familiar touch or an occasional kiss, anything to signify a change, but no. Certainly there were times during the day when she caught him watching her with an overheated gaze, but when their glances would lock, his always shifted away.

A woman like Gillian would know how to approach the situation, but Brooke wasn't ready to divulge her feelings about the Captain to Gillian because then Brooke would have to explain why she was working for the Captain and she expected that a woman as sophisticated as Gillian wouldn't appreciate the personal satisfaction in heavy manual labor. Second, Brooke suspected that Gillian wouldn't approve of having sex with the man who was providing both a roof and paycheck. Last, and most important, Brooke knew that although the Captain had many feelings for her, he never said anything that implied a romantic relationship. Other than the long, deep kisses, or the way he made her ache between her legs, all of which were not things that Brooke felt comfortable divulging to anyone, much less her future sister-in-law who was mostly a stranger and engaged to Brooke's brother, who was even more of a stranger. No, the situation needed patience and strategy, and Brooke, who had previously been unable to strategize her way out of a paper bag, was starting to learn.

That afternoon, she sorted rubber gaskets and devised a plan to move their relationship to a higher level. The Captain had his truck parked near the black metal gate, unloading the widow Kenley's broken washing machine. Mouth dry, she admired his broad build, the firm thighs. However, this was about moving their relationship beyond the sex.

After she cleared the fog from her eyes, she went over and planted herself at the foot of the truck. "I need your advice," she began, trying to sound earnest and composed and not remotely aroused. "Rita likes me," she continued. "The Hinkles have forgiven me since I helped Henry haul a case of milk to the refrigerator in the back. I'm making good progress at creating a bond with these people."

"Then there's no problem. You don't need my advice."

"Sure I do. Gillian invited me to the chili cook-off on

Friday. She said I should go and make some new friends. I think it's a good idea."

The Captain climbed down from the back of his truck and dusted his palms on his jeans. "I don't know any chili recipes."

Usually the Captain was much more cooperative when she came to him for help. Usually he was more than ready to offer advice, even when she didn't want to hear it, but today he'd been unusually distant. Acknowledging that this was going to be more difficult than she assumed, she approached the situation from a different angle. "It's Austen."

This time he frowned. "Is he giving you problems?"

Brooke shrugged helplessly. "He's not acting brotherly. It's like he's scared of me. Gillian doesn't seem scared of me. I don't understand why Austen is."

Now that he knew neither chili nor social niceties were involved, the Captain pulled off his cap, pushed his fingers through his hair, messing it up even more. Brooke longed to touch the thick strands, fix it for him, but relationship novice or not, she knew this wasn't the time.

"Why should he be scared of you? You don't look that tough. He'd take you down in one."

"Be serious," she scoffed, sliding into an easy camaraderie, a casual banter.

"I was," he said, slapping the cap on his head. Before he could go back to work, she jumped up on the lowered tailgate and sat. At first, he looked ready to cut her off again. Brooke fixed him with her earnest face, which wasn't threatening at all.

"Do you have any brothers or sisters?" she asked.

His mouth quirked at the corners, almost a smile. "There's seven of us."

Seven? Good heavens. "Where are they?"

"George is a chemist in Rockville. David is in California,

somewhere outside L.A. Sara teaches kindergarten in Baltimore. John's a bartender in Miami. Robert's still in the army and, to be honest, I don't know where the hell Charlie is living now. He does consulting for some company with a lot of initials and I lost track."

"What about your father?"

"My dad lives with Sara. He likes to help out, so he does some of her repairs, and helps her with her kids."

"Do you see him often?"

"No."

"Why?"

The Captain shrugged, as if this was normal.

"Do you not get along?"

"We get along great. We talk almost every week. It's just…"

"What?"

He shrugged again. "I don't know."

"What about your brothers?"

"I see them some. Four years ago I flew up to Maryland for the holidays."

"Impressive," she murmured.

"We get along great," he repeated, more defensively this time.

"Excellent. Then you must know how brothers are supposed to act."

The Captain glanced at the washing machine, then back at Brooke. Resigned to the conversation, he climbed up on the tailgate and sat next to her, their thighs almost touching, but not quite. Definite progress. "There's not a manual."

Brooke sighed because it wasn't that she expected the Captain to be a fount of family how-to knowledge, but still… He was very smart.

"Why is he scared of me?" she asked, looking away. She didn't want him to think that people might not like her. However, he must have heard the unhappiness in her voice, because he took her hand as if he liked her. For the Captain, hand-holding was way beyond easy camaraderie. It was right up there with poetry writing and mix-tapes.

"I don't think he's scared."

"What do you think it is?" she asked, meeting his eyes, not so worried about hiding her uncertainty. This was all uncharted territory for Brooke. Family. A respectful relationship with a man. Home. She'd spent her whole life dreaming of something like this, and now it was within her grasp, unless she fumbled it all away. Charlene Hart was a world-class fumbler.

Seeing the frown on her face, the Captain squeezed her hand. "I don't know what his problem is. I barely know the guy and it's not like I've seen the two of you together."

"Come to the cook-off," she pressed. "Tell me what I'm doing wrong."

"I'm not going to a chili cook-off," he muttered, and while he didn't look thrilled at the idea, he didn't look stubborn, either. Brooke allowed herself a tiny squeeze on his hand, as well.

"Please? I don't know how to do this, and I don't want to mess it up." Yes, she was talking about more than her brother, and she suspected he knew. Once again, he didn't look thrilled at the idea, but he didn't look stubborn, either.

"I'll go," he agreed.

Progress. Definitely.

THE TIN CUP CHILI-PALOOZA was scheduled for the Friday of homecoming weekend. The week before, the town hung a banner across Main Street that read, Go Lions, Maul Midland, as if the Tin Cup high school football team was not going to get eaten alive by the state's powerhouse.

However, Brooke seemed excited, and the night of the

hell-a-palooza she changed outfits four times, all the more
telling since Jason knew she only had three to begin with.
Not wanting to disappoint her, Jason told her that the red
sundress was the best. He neglected to mention that her
legs were starting to get a mouth-watering tan, that the
modified-transistors hanging from her ears looked cute
next to the slender curve of her neck, and then there was
the way she wasn't wearing a bra.

Three weeks ago, when Brooke had first come to town,
the idea of Brooke not wearing a bra was sexy, but not so
irresistible that he wanted to jump her. Jason told himself
that the fact that he *had* jumped her was due to his own
long months of monklike celibacy, which had killed whatever restraint he normally possessed. Tonight, his restraint
was threatening to bust his jeans, since now that she had
put on a little weight, the hollows in her cheeks were gone,
and apparently when Brooke gained weight, it went to her
breasts.

He closed his good eye—didn't work. When he opened
it again, they were still going, and Brooke was bouncy,
cheery, nipples pebbling against the flimsy material.

During the daylight hours he worked very hard to keep
from touching her, but right now, all he wanted to do was
push the dress aside, put his mouth to her, pull up her skirt,
while the long, tan legs wrapped around...

"What do you think?" she asked, twirling in front of
him, the skirt floating dangerously high.

Jason reached for the tools on his kitchen table, found
a screwdriver, and jammed the metal head into his palm.
Better. "It's okay."

At his half-hearted comment, Brooke stopped her twirling abruptly. "Okay? That's all?"

Realizing that, yes, he'd disappointed her again, Jason
tried to make amends, while not sounding like a man with

a raging hard-on that didn't give a damn about a dress. "Pretty," he told her.

Instantly her smile bloomed, and once again she twirled like a kid, her red high-heels clicking on the old floors. "Thank you," she said, and planted a kiss on his cheek.

The cheek kisses were becoming standard. He wasn't sure whether they were supposed to be sexual or paternal. In his mind, little girls kissed their grandparents on the cheek, but when Brooke kissed him, her lips stayed on his skin one second longer than seemed proper, her mouth a little more slack than what Jason thought paternal entailed. It was a lot easier to blame her kissing skills for the steel in his cock, rather than this own dirty mind, but no matter how hard he tried to erase the image, his mind always came back to one naked Brooke Hart.

Her chest brushed against him.

"You look pretty, too," she said, eyes lingering on his face.

Jason laughed, glad to not think about one naked Brooke Hart. "I'm not pretty."

Her fingers brushed at his unruly hair, traced the line of his freshly shaven, thankfully un-nicked jaw. "You are to me," she said, her voice soft and floaty, and he didn't want to justify her foolishness with a smile. It would only encourage the foolishness, but he smiled anyway.

"We'll take two cars tonight. You're trying to be respectable and people will talk if I drive you home."

"You think they might guess that we're doing the nasty?" she teased, and he didn't want to be teased. Not while he kept picturing her skirt around her waist.

"Can we not talk about this?" he said, putting his screwdriver away, forcing his good eye off her legs.

"I'd like to talk about it," she said, and his good eye wandered back to her legs, up over her cherry nipples.

"Where are your car keys?" he asked, his voice polite and sensible.

"I hid them." She tilted her head, long hair falling around her shoulders. "Want to know where?"

"No."

"Then we'll have to take your truck. I can sit close if you'd like and you can slip your hand up my skirt."

Jason swallowed, feeling his jeans start to cut off his blood flow, only a good thing. He didn't like this flirty, butterfly Brooke. He didn't like to think about slipping his hand up her skirt. "Have you been drinking?"

"Nope. Not a lick." Her mouth curved up, and tonight it was extra red, extra glossy, extra wet. *Hell.* Jason took a step back.

"You can't do this at the cook-off. If you want Austen to like you, you can't be picking up strange men and having sex with them."

"You're not a strange man. You're very normal." She took a step forward, her hand sliding over his fly. Jason bit through his tongue. "Wonderfully normal."

Regrettably, he removed her hand. "Brooke."

She moved an inch closer. "Captain."

Sweat pooled at the back of his neck. "We need to leave."

"Why?" she asked, so close that he could feel the burn of her breasts.

"You don't want to be late," he explained, very logical, very rational, all while some odd perfume was seducing his nose.

"Better to be late than early." Not content with nose-seduction, she unbuttoned the top button on his shirt, pressing a possessive kiss to his chest. When she raised her head, there was a bright red lipstick mark on his chest. Definitely not a grandfather kiss.

His hands reached out to grasp her hips and move her

away, but accidentally landed underneath her skirt, discovering nothing but hot skin and a tiny thong.

"Captain," she whispered, her voice shocked and shameless, exactly like in every porn movie ever made. "What are you doing?"

"Looking for your car keys."

She raised a brow and wiggled beneath his clumsy hands. "Very clever. Do you think they'll guess?"

Of course they would guess. They would see the lust in his eyes, they would see the way his fingers were always reaching in her direction. They would see the world's most obvious hard-on in his jeans. "You're going to hate yourself if you ruin your chances with Austen." Even while he was warning her, his thumb was stroking the slit between her legs, feeling the swollen skin already damp with desire.

She closed her eyes, and he heard a pleased hum in her throat. When she opened them again, the longing there shocked him. "I like seeing you like this, crisp white shirt, no ballcap to hide your hair. You have great hair, like old copper, but soft, touchable." Her fingers tangled there. "You should get dressed up more often."

The wistful comment only cemented his belief that Brooke, much like every other woman, wanted a traditional man with a traditional job in a traditional house, but his cementlike beliefs didn't stop his hands from staying between her legs, finding her slick, swollen and traditionally aroused.

When his finger slid inside her, she gasped, small crooked teeth clutching her lower lip. He knew just how that lower lip felt. "We're going to be late," he warned, feeling his restraint slip away. "You might mess up your dress. And think of all the time you spent getting it just right."

"Save the dress," she ordered with a laugh.

Not giving her a chance to change her mind, Jason fisted

the material in his hand, raised the dress higher, until he could see the bare legs, the strapping red heels, and the tiny red scrap of silk.

No, there wasn't a woman alive who was hotter, livelier, more giving than Brooke Hart, and although he knew her infatuation wasn't going to last, he still wanted this. Part of him knew he had to be careful with her dress and he turned her around, bent her over the back of the couch, her dark hair falling low down the slender curve of her back. His hungry gaze traced over the ripe curves of her ass, and she was completely relaxed, completely trusting that he wouldn't hurt her at all. Quickly he unzipped his fly, sheathed himself and then slid between her cheeks, pushing higher, watching her body arch in response.

"I'll be careful," he promised, his voice tough as nails, and he leaned over her, sliding loose one shoulder of her dress, baring her breast. She took his calloused palm, cupped it over the flawless skin, sighing as his thumb rolled back and forth over those cheery nipples that had mocked him earlier.

Slowly, ever so carefully he filled her, listening to her quiet sighs of pleasure, feeling her heart race under his hand.

Dog rolled closer, the red eyes unblinking, unseeing, but still accusing, and Jason swore.

Brooke turned her head, met his eyes and laughed. It was a great laugh, filled with life and joy, and Jason didn't want to laugh back, but he did.

She leaned lower, hips tilted higher, and Jason wanted to swear again because this was not gentle and careful. He closed his good eye, but he could feel the clench of her muscles around him. He could smell her sex, and he moved faster, plunging deeper inside her, fingers pulling at the fragile material of her dress.

Her head lolled, her breathing as hard and as fast as his cock. Her hand squeezed his, pressing hard into the soft tissue of her breast. His ham-fisted fingers tightened and twisted on her skin, her dress, and he drove her even faster, not gentle, not careful. He could hear her words, nonsense, and her hips moved with him, making this too easy, too good. Wanting to feel her come around him, his free hand slid between the front of her thighs, stroking her where they were joined. *Temporary,* he reminded himself. *Only sex.*

"Please," she gasped, and his finger pressed hard against her clit, telling himself it was only sex. Instantly she froze, smooth legs locked against him. Long shudders racked her body, and unable to resist, he pushed aside her hair and pressed one small kiss on her neck. Her skin smelled like perfume, rich and exotic. Perfume mixed with sex. Rich, exotic sex.

The kind of sex that was never enough. Jason thrust one last time, nothing rich, nothing exotic. As he spilled himself into the condom, his fingers clenched, and the fragile material of her dress split into pieces.

There was a second afterward when he didn't want to leave her, when his hand refused to release the soft skin of her breast, but it was that quiet ripping sound that jerked him back to reality. That and the stiffening of her shoulder, the way she didn't meet his eyes.

Quickly he withdrew, pushed the ruined fabric down over the dream of her hips and cleaned himself up.

She turned, examined the torn dress, and then looked at him as if nothing was wrong.

"I'm sorry," he apologized, but she waved it off.

"It doesn't matter. I liked the jeans and shirt better. Let me change, find my keys, and after that we can go. And look, not too late after all."

9

THERE WERE CERTAIN indignities that a man wasn't supposed to endure, namely any TV show with Housewives in the title, bubble baths or competing for an apron that said "Kiss the Cook."

Tables lined the high school parking lot, covered with sterno pans and red-checkered cloths. The air was filled with the scent of peppers because everybody knew that if the late afternoon sun wasn't hot enough to kill you, then the food should. Jason arrived a good fifteen minutes behind Brooke, not that it mattered since he picked her out of the crowd right away.

Even in jeans and a yellow button-down she was gorgeous, dark hair waving around her face, dreamy eyes that saw life better than it was. No, in Brooke's world, jeans were just as nice as a ripped sundress.

For a man who had seen a lot of bad, a ripped sundress shouldn't be eating at his gut. Jason told himself not to dwell on ripped sundresses or past mistakes. No, for tonight, all would do was buy himself a beer, find an unoccupied lawn chair, and pretend that he could dissolve into the ground.

After he'd found an isolated spot, Austen Hart dragged

a chair over and clinked his bottle. Obviously Jason was failing at pretty much everything today.

"Howdy, neighbor! Gotta say you look like you're having a hell of a time. Got some chili in the competition?"

Jason stared with his one good eye. "Do I look like I wear an apron?"

"Didn't think so. Me, neither. I'm just here for the free beer because the bartender likes me." Austen waved at the older woman who was pulling beer from the cooler in the back of her truck, who promptly waved back. "Gillian warned me not to get liquored up, but I'm thinking that several cold beers is the only way to escape judging this event."

"Got that right," Jason agreed, and then realized if he acted too miserable, Brooke's older brother was going to wonder why Jason even bothered to come at all. Because he was a sap. That was why he bothered to come.

He had come to help her. That was why he was here. Once he'd pulled his face into some semblance of cheerfulness, he waded into the conversation that he thought would help Brooke. "How's it going with your relative? Who'd you say was visiting? Your brother, your sister? Ah, hell, I don't remember. Who's the relative?"

"Little sis. That's her over there." Austen pointed his bottle in the direction of the woman who only minutes ago Jason had bent over his couch. Oh, not the time to think about sex. Really, really not the time. Discreetly Jason moved his bottle lower in his lap.

"She looks like a nice kid," he commented innocently.

Austen shook his head sadly. "I think that's the problem."

"Why?"

"She looks so normal, so ordinary, so average. My

old man, well, let's just say things were very not normal, and...I don't know."

"What?" prompted Jason, now curious.

"You really care?"

Quickly Jason backtracked because he didn't want to care and most of all, he didn't want Brooke or Austen to know that he did. "It's either listening to you or taste-testing chili and possibly revisiting the experience for the next five days. I think your family history sounds fascinating."

"I like you, Jackson," Austen told him, taking another swallow of beer.

"It's Jason."

Austen clicked his tongue. "Oh, yeah. The Captain. Were you a captain in the service?"

"Staff sergeant."

Brooke's brother threw back his head and laughed, and Jason noticed Brooke looking curiously in their direction. Jason looked away.

"And how did that turn into captain?" Austen asked, and it seemed only fair to give the guy the truth.

"My ex didn't like being married to a staff sergeant, so she told her aunt and uncle that I was a captain, and it stuck."

"It's better than Sarge."

"True," he acknowledged, and then steered the conversation away from himself. He was here to help Brooke. Help her establish a relationship with her brother, help her find a better place to stay. Yeah, he was here to help her, absolutely nothing more.

Jason took a sip of beer, then kicked back in his chair, looking as thoughtful and wise as a one-eyed man could be. "I have a lot of brothers and sisters, and we were never that close, but family is important. I mean, I have one brother, Richard, and he's a total ass, but he's family and I have to stick by him. You need to stick by your sister, too." It wasn't the truth, but the lie was for the greater good. Lately, he'd been justifying a lot by the greater good, which smacked of bullshit, but what the hell.

"I'll stick by her as long as she's in town."

Austen talked as if Brooke Hart was temporary. "Maybe she'll want to settle here."

"I don't think so. She's a city girl, used to neon lights, high-dollar shopping and spa treatments involving mud."

Was Austen really that blind? Hell, Jason was at fifty percent vision, and even he knew that was wrong. "She doesn't look like a city girl to me."

"Appearances can be deceiving. Besides, every woman is a high-dollar shopper."

"Including the future missus?"

Austen laughed again. "Gillian just wants people to think that. Although she does pay more for a haircut than I pay for a suit."

"She seems nice, your future missus—for an officer of the law."

"Thanks." Austen studied Jason and the laid-back expression was gone, his eyes a little sharper than before. "You were married to one of the Hinkles?"

"Sonya."

"Oh, yeah. She was a cheerleader when I was a freshman."

Jason held up his hand. "Don't tell me any more."

"I was only going to say that she seemed nice."

"She's okay."

"The bloom's off the rose?"

"I was never a rose. I think she wanted a rose." Jason took a long drink of cold beer, realizing that what she'd done didn't bother him so much anymore.

"Sucks."

"Nah. I don't think it would have lasted anyway. We spent more time apart than together."

Austen considered that for a second. "Don't you get lonely out there?"

Jason's first instinct was to lie, but he liked Brooke's brother, and so he settled on the truth. "Maybe."

"You should get out more. Go to Smitty's and get a beer. I'll tell Ernestine that you're a friend and she'll set you up with a free drink. You know, the town's not too bad. Not that there's a lot of women in Tin Cup, but there's some. I could ask Gillian to ask around. She knows everybody."

Jason coughed suddenly. "Not in the market."

"Probably smart. If you change your mind..."

Across the parking lot, Gillian Wanamaker strode onto the stage and Jason noticed the way Austen stopped talking and drinking to stare. Then the mayor shuffled up the stairs and stood next to her, and Austen resumed the conversation again. "You ever watch football?"

"The Redskins. Not a popular choice in Texas."

"Did you grow up in D.C.?"

"Maryland, around Baltimore."

"All right, I'll let it slide, but don't tell anybody, will you? Trust me, people in this town don't ever forget."

On the stage, Gillian raised a longneck high. "Ladies and gentleman, children of all ages, it's finally happened! Mark your calendars because three weeks from now, a mere ten days before my wedding, the mayor will be breaking ground on the new train station, and I want all y'all to come out and watch the future of Tin Cup begin to unfold. As you know, none of this would have been possible without Austen Hart, and I'd like everyone to raise a glass, because the Hart name means something to this town, not just to me. To Austen."

Bottles clinked. There were a few cheers and just as

many boos, but Austen laughed good-naturedly and looked at Jason. "Like I said, they got a long memory in this town, and if they know you're a Redskins fan, you're dead."

It wasn't his football loyalties that bothered Jason the most. Although she was pretending not to look, Jason could see Brooke staring at her brother, so much loneliness in her face. "I bet she'd like it if you spoke to her. You know, like a brother. She seems a little lost."

"Brooke?"

Jason tried to sound astoundingly innocent. "Oh, is that her name?"

"Yeah. Brooke Hart."

"Then you should go over and talk." Jason sipped his beer and then nodded wisely. "It's family. It's what you do."

LATER THAT NIGHT, the crickets were out and somewhere a coyote was howling at the moon. An ordinary Texas night, except for the bubbling chatter of the woman sitting next to Jason on the porch.

"I think he's coming around. He didn't act too nervous, and even asked which chili I thought was the best."

"None of the chili was the best. What happened to hot-dog eating, or pie eating or even turkey legs? Chili is just a recipe for disaster."

"You're making a funny, aren't you?"

"Bad chili is nothing to joke about."

"Did you have a good time?"

"Sucked," he told her, but he smiled and she knew he was lying, and he didn't mind.

Repeating her brother's words, she told him, "You should do more. Get out more."

He leaned back on the seat, stretched his legs in front of him. "Why? If there's one place in the world that God meant for man to be alone, it's here." In complete contradiction to that statement, Jason moved his foot to press the tiny button at the base of the swing. Instantly, the canopy netting was full of twinkling lights like a thousand fireflies brightening up the night.

Jason watched, fascinated with the excited glow in her eyes, the bubble of laughter in her throat. For Brooke, everything was new and wonderful. He was going to miss this. He was going to miss her. She pressed her lips to his cheek, to his mouth, and he felt his body stir.

In the scarred remains of his heart, he knew that she wanted more. He knew she wanted the life that she'd never had. He knew that not encouraging her infatuation was the right thing to do, the honorable thing to do, but it didn't stop his hands from tangling in her hair, from him feeding on her mouth, from pulling her into his lap with a thousand fireflies twinkling behind her in the sky.

The right thing wasn't supposed to hurt. The right thing had never hurt before. Hardly anything had ever hurt before. It was a helluva bad time to start getting sensitive now.

And that was what he told himself when she undressed under the lonely Texas moon, when she impaled herself on his cock and he watched her dark eyes as he moved inside her, and no matter the bright watts burning overhead, it was only her that he could see.

WHEN IT CAME TO FAMILY, Gillian Wanamaker followed strict Emily Post protocols, and no matter how fast Austen wanted to run away from his sister, Gillian believed that in the end, Brooke's wistful smile and brand-new boots were bound to win him over. After all, not that he would ever admit it, but Austen Hart was a soft-touch.

And in the interim, when Austen didn't conform to Gillian's ideals of hospitable behavior, Gillian would fill the void with a visit and some snicker-doodles and mini-pies.

Since she was on a mission, and wanted to be casual, she dragged her best friend, Mindy, along.

"Now remember, she's family and doesn't know a soul, so be nice."

Mindy folded her arms over her post-baby stomach. "I'm always nice, Gillian Wanamaker. The post-partum hormones might have taken over my body, but they can't steal the mind."

"I'm rambling. I'm nervous."

"And why in Sam Hill are you nervous? Don't make me call you silly Gilly again. Once in a lifetime is enough."

Gillian slid her sheriff's cruiser into the inn's parking lot and scanned the scene. Then swore.

"What?"

"She's not here," Gillian deduced, then glanced over her shoulder, looking at the cute autumnal baskets stacked neatly in front of her shotgun and Kevlar vest. "Let's go ahead and taken them in. The chocolate is going to die in the heat, and what sort of sister-in-law gives out melted chocolate?"

"Delores will eat those suckers up if you leave them at the front desk with her."

Good point. Gillian considered it for a minute. "Unless I pick up the hotel phone and leave a voice message in Brooke's room saying that the basket is at the front desk, and making sure that Delores can hear."

"She could delete the message."

"She's not that smart."

Mindy met her eyes. "You're right. Hormones again."

Sure enough, inside the Spotlight Inn, Delores was working the desk.

"Girl, look at you," Gillian gushed. "I swear, you get prettier all the time. You've lost weight, haven't you?"

Delores smoothed the blouse over her definitely trimmer stomach. "Weight Watchers. Down nine pounds in four months."

Gillian pumped her fist in the air. "You go, girl."

Right then, Delores noticed the basket. "That sure is kind of you, but sweets are taboo."

Gillian laughed, one of those "I'm such a ditz" laughs. "Actually, I brought it in for Austen's sister, Brooke. Cute little thing. Walks around like she's a bit lost. I didn't see her car in the lot, but you tell me which room she's in and I can plop this on her bed. Maybe add a little note."

"Who?" Delores looked at her blankly, and although the desk clerk had many faults, she *always* knew her paying customers.

Mindy started to talk, but Gillian nudged her in the side. "Did she not check in yet? I could've sworn that Austen said she was staying here."

Delores shook her head. "No reservation. All we got is four dentists from Abilene and the railroad surveying crew from Austin. That one foreman is kinda hot. Too bad you're taken."

Gillian flashed her ring, which she was in a habit of doing, which her mama always told her was ostentatious, but Gillian believed that a newly engaged woman should be a little ostentatious, unless she wasn't in true love, which Gillian most definitely was. "Listen, if you see Brooke, don't tell her I stopped by. I want this to be a surprise."

"Do you want me to call you when she checks in?"

"Do you mind? I want to make sure she feels right at home."

Delores saluted. "On the case, Sheriff."

Once they were outside, Mindy started in. "What's going on?"

For a moment, Gillian pondered this new dilemma. "I sent her here, but I don't know that's where she landed."

"Where else could she go?"

"Nowhere."

"Call her," Mindy suggested. "Tell her you have a surprise. Trap her in a lie."

"Now calm down, Mindy. There's been no lying. She's family and besides that, she doesn't have a cell."

"Who doesn't have a cell?"

"My great-aunt Cora doesn't have a cell."

"She's nearly eighty."

"Doesn't matter. It's not that strange."

"It's strange," Mindy pronounced, and privately Gillian agreed, but right now she needed to look unconcerned.

"I'll drop you back at your house, then I need to make an appearance at the courthouse."

Mindy looked at her, disappointed. "I thought this was a mission."

"Doesn't Brandon have a two o'clock feeding? You're going to let that poor baby starve?"

Mindy sighed. "It's very difficult being a mother."

"Tell it to the hand, sweetie. Tell it to the hand."

TWO HOURS LATER, Gillian was still combing the town for a beat-up Impala that should have stood out like not only a sore but bruised, beaten and banged-up thumb.

But there was no Impala to be found. At that point, Gillian grabbed her radio, prepared to issue an APB for the missing vehicle, but official sheriff directives meant official paperwork, and official records. Gillian's gut told her that official records were never a good idea where family was concerned. So, she drove down Main, turned at Pecos, past the drive-in, across the interstate and even wandered across the county line. Still no Impala.

Actually, in a fine twist of fate and logic, it wasn't until she'd abandoned her search that she found it. As she was heading over to Austen's house, she happened to glance at the old Hinkle place, and lo and behold, there among the sheds and tires and tubs and two-by-fours sat an Impala as if it belonged there.

Gillian knew her town and she knew who lived there. Sonya Hinkle's ex, Jason Kincaid. Sonya had been an over-achiever in high school, two years older than Gillian, with that Hollywood platinum hair that Gillian had secretly coveted until she found out that Sonya was driving into Austin to get her hair colored every two months.

According to official records, Jason was thirty-four years old. Staff sergeant with the U.S. Army, honorably discharged when he lost his left eye. He was a loner, who liked to pick up scrap metal and parts. Suspected in the gifting of a lawn mower for the Strickland landscaping company, an industrial strength dryer for the homeless shelter at the church and a large wooden pirate ship for the elementary school. All allegations were unproven and since he went to so much trouble to keep his good deeds quiet, Gillian chose not to reveal that the set of prints on the dryer came back a ten-point match.

So, why was Brooke parked at the house? Maybe she knew him from New York, Iraq...*here?*

Gillian drummed her fingers on the steering wheel, sizing up the situation, knowing that it required some discreet snooping around, of which she was something of a professional.

Her mouth pulled into a thoughtful frown, and she shifted the car into Reverse. She'd get her facts in a row, and when she did, she'd tell Austen, but she'd have to craft the moment exactly right.

First, a little moonlight Hart-house demolition to lift his mood. Next, a long bout of Austen Hart loving. Then, when he was lying next to her, sated, happy and full of the intangible wonderment of their emotional connection, she'd tell him that his little sister had hooked up with the Captain.

Who woulda thunk it? Little sister worked fast.

10

Brooke was leaving Hinkle's grocery when Gillian rushed toward her, pulling her into a big hug. Brooke froze, then quickly returned the hug before Gillian thought something was wrong.

"Hey, sis! What are you doing?" Gillian took Brooke's sack of food in her arms, then led her down Main, past Dot's diner, past the What in Carnation flower shop, past the fence in front of the Presbyterian church until they were standing at the park located next to the base of the courthouse steps, Lady Liberty watching Brooke skeptically.

Brooke managed a smile. "I should get my food back to the hotel before it goes bad."

Gillian pushed her down on a wooden bench and then plopped down next to her, her sheriff's badge blinding in its glare. Brooke wasn't used to seeing Gillian in uniform and to tell the truth, the badge and the gun made her nervous. Still, this was Gillian, one of the nicest, friendliest people Brooke had ever met. There was no reason to be nervous.

Lady Liberty glared. Brooke gulped.

"You don't have any perishables in there, do you?" Gillian asked, watching Brooke with those clear blue eyes that saw all. "I know there's none of those mini-fridges at the Inn. I love those things. Don't you love those things, with those little candied almonds, but gah-ah-ly, can you believe what the big cities charge for them? Being from New York, you know all about those mini-fridges, don't you?"

Oh, God. She knew. Brooke tried an innocent expression and knew she'd failed. She'd never been very good at the art of deception, folding under pressure like a cheap suit. "I was planning on telling you and Austen the truth."

Gillian cocked her head, giving her an understanding smile. "Did you think we would care? Now, I know that some people stand in judgment in this tiny pill of a town, but, sweetie, we're family, and you don't have to keep secrets from Austen and me."

Brooke's shoulders slumped from the relief of it. "All I wanted was for him to like me."

Gillian frowned. "That's so sweet. Of course he likes you—doesn't he?"

Brooke frowned. "Don't you know?"

Gillian's clear blue eyes narrowed. Now she looked like a cop. "What are we talking about?"

"What are you talking about?"

"You and Jason, carrying on. Gotta say, you don't let any grass grow under your feet. But if that's not what we're discussing, then what are we discussing?"

Brooke blinked, trying for guileless. "The Captain, of course."

Gillian leaned back on the bench, and laid an arm across Brooke's shoulders. It should have been comforting. It was a trap. "Brooke, first of all, I think you're cute as a button with those darling little puppy-dog eyes, but not only am I a trained law enforcement professional, I love Austen Hart, and don't think I would hesitate to break your face into little puppy dog pieces if there's anything that you're hiding from him that would hurt him. Unless he's not your brother?"

Gillian smiled with even white teeth. It was a beautiful smile. Brooke wasn't fooled.

The other woman was breathing fire, overly protective, fiercely loyal, just like families were supposed to be. Something Charlene Hart had never learned, and something Brooke desperately needed. Maybe it was time to tell the truth. Maybe all that over-protective loyalty would cover sins of poverty and omission, as well.

"I did what I did because I wanted Tyler and Austen to like me. They don't know me, and I don't think they like me."

"You took Austen's mother away from him and his brother. She left them and traded in for a better life in New York. You got a great stepfather, they got Frank Hart. Sweetheart, it doesn't matter if you were sitting in your mama's stomach when she left. You could be the most perfect sister ever and he'd still have issues. Now what are you not telling me?"

Brooke took a deep breath. "I don't have a stepfather."

"You lied?"

"Yes."

"If that wasn't your stepfather's house in New York when the boys visited, then whose was it? Your mother's?"

"I don't know who it belonged to. There was an open house. I bribed a Realtor to let me use it for a couple of hours."

"Where was your real home?" asked Gillian, looking not so threatening, not so judgmental.

"I didn't have one."

Gillian's mouth curved into an indulgent smile. "Of course you did. Maybe it wasn't some hoity-toity mansion in New York, but everybody has a home."

Carefully Brooke met her eyes. "Not everyone."

It took Gillian only a few seconds to comprehend, and pity flashed in her eyes. "I'm sorry. It must have been very hard on you and your mother."

Gillian was inviting her to tell some hugely sorrowful tales about life on the streets, just like most people did when confronted with a homeless person. Charlene Hart had thrived on her hard-luck stories, but not so much Brooke. "Austen and Tyler didn't miss very much when they were growing up without their mother."

"A family isn't about money or a house. It's not like they were rolling in it, either. They wouldn't have cared if Charlene Hart was poor or not."

"They might care if she had substance abuse problems."

Gillian's mouth drew into a little "oh" of enlightenment. "You should know your father Frank was a drunk, a vile SOB with a mouth as bitter as his black heart. Sounds like your mother was no prize, but that's all on Frank and Charlene, not you, not Austen, not Tyler. I've never known three people more determined to pretend that everything's fine. It's not, but now you three have each other, so the secrets have got to stop. You have to tell Austen. I'll keep quiet for a couple of days because it needs to come from you, but I won't keep it forever. Lies have a way of coming out, and people get hurt. I won't let him get hurt. His father has already hurt him enough."

Easy words from a woman who had lived a normal life, but there was a certainty in Gillian's face that inspired Brooke and made her want to believe Gillian. There would be a remarkable freedom in knowing that the pretense was over. All her life she'd pretended, but maybe Gillian was right.

Eventually Brooke nodded. "I'll do it."

Gillian patted her on the shoulder, as if everything would

be okay. Brooke liked that about her future sister-in-law. Her confidence in the future. Of course, people who had a home usually did have that confidence. And now Brooke had a home, too. Or at least part of one. Slowly she smiled.

"And since we're family now, tell me all about Jason," Gillian prodded. "How the heck did that happen?"

"He gave me a job."

At the words, Gillian's eyes widened with shock. "What sort of job?" Then she held up a hand. "Nope. If there's illegal shenanigans going on, I don't want to know." She paused. "No, no, that's not right. As your future sister-in-law, I have to know if you have a life in crime."

Brooke laughed. "There's no crime. He's paying me to organize his parts."

Gillian's cop-look was back. "Parts?"

"You've seen his land. He has a lot of parts. He doesn't know what he owns. I'm grouping things together and writing it down."

"But you're living there."

Sometimes people missed the obvious. "I couldn't afford the motel."

"Oh." Gillian nodded. "Oh. I thought you were...you know."

Brooke felt a hot flush on her cheeks, but hopefully Gillian wouldn't notice. "He's very nice, but I don't think he sees me that way." It was a modified version of the truth. A version that would meet with the Captain's approval.

"You like him?"

Brooke nodded.

Gillian rolled her eyes. "Well, then I don't know what's wrong with the man."

Brooke liked the sympathy, the unwavering support. Family. It was nice. "It's all right. I've got enough on my mind right now."

"You come stay with us," Gillian offered, because of course Gillian would offer Brooke a place to stay. It was the next logical step, and Brooke wanted to whack her head against the bench for not thinking ahead.

"You don't have enough room in your house. You have Austen. Your parents. I'm perfectly comfortable where I am." It was a good answer, the one that made Brooke's situation seem reasonable, however, Gillian was not to be dissuaded.

"We have a sleeper sofa and a blow-up…" She stopped, swore. "Stupid me. We'll get you a room at the Spotlight. You don't have to stay with Jason. Austen and I will pick up the tab. That way you can have some privacy and a place of your own. It'll be temporary until the lawyer gets back and the papers are signed, but I bet you'll love it."

"That's very kind," started Brooke, "but—"

Gillian gave her arm a friendly squeeze. "No buts, sweetie. You're family."

HAVING DIFFICULT conversations was not one of Brooke's strengths, and because any conversation with the Captain was a difficult conversation, having this particular difficult conversation was not something she knew how to do.

Leaving here would be like cutting off an arm, or a leg, or a heart.… She wiped at her tears, because the last thing she wanted was to bust out bawling in front of him before the conversation even started. Every time she looked around the house, she could feel the sting in her heart.

Outside was even worse. Such a beautiful place, and no one would ever see it the way she did. The practical shade netting was like a twinkling night sky. The swinging bench seat on the porch was the literal Cadillac of porch swings, perfect for watching the sun wake to the world. The cactus she'd placed in the window was sturdy and immoveable, not only decorative, but able to survive and thrive. All of these little things were home.

Most of all, the Captain felt like home, which was why Brooke was avoiding the conversation like the plague. Eventually, it was late afternoon, and if Brooke wasn't at the hotel by dark, Gillian would know there was a problem and the Captain would realize that Brooke hadn't told him she was leaving, and then the Captain would wonder why she hadn't told him that she was leaving, surmising that Brooke didn't want to leave and hadn't planned on telling him—which was exactly the reason.

This sort of strategic, long-term thinking was smart and needed to be done, but that didn't mean it hurt any less. There was no way that the Captain would invite her to stay if she had other options and now Brooke had other options. More than anything, she wanted more time, but since it was now three o'clock and she had piddled away another seven minutes by thinking, time wasn't a luxury that Brooke could afford.

After changing into her favorite white tank top, she made her face look presentable. She brushed her hair until it shone because she knew the Captain loved her hair. When ready, she appeared outside where the Captain was rolling the widow Kenley's washing machine into the bed of his truck and slamming the tailgate closed. Determined to get this over with, Brooke swung open the passenger door of the truck and planted herself on the seat.

After he got behind the wheel, the Captain, to his credit, didn't tell her to get out, but instead shifted to face her, giving her the full-on pirate stare—a feeble attempt at intimidation. "Why are you here?"

"You can't lift the washing machine out by yourself," Brooke pointed out.

"Sure, I can. How do you think I got it here? Little elves?"

Trying another tactic, she rolled down the window, propped her elbow on the door, feeling the sun warm on her arm. "It's a great day. I'd love to go for a drive."

She could feel the touch of his gaze skimming over her chest, her mouth, and she knew what lay behind that look, but yes, this was the Captain. "You'll get sunburned."

"Are you ashamed to be seen with me?" It was a cheap shot, worthy of Charlene Hart, but Brooke had tried logic and seduction, and if pity was all she had left, well, so be it.

The Captain muttered something obscene. "It's not you. You're beautiful and smart and you make people want to be around you. No man in his right mind would be ashamed to be seen with you."

It was the most extravagant thing he'd ever said. He thought she was beautiful, a word she hadn't been sure was in his vocabulary. "Really? You're not just saying that to be nice?"

"I don't say anything just to be nice."

"Yes, you do," she corrected. "You don't like anybody to know that you do, but you do."

"Why are you here? I know there's a reason. What it is, I don't know, but I know it's going to scare me."

If it had been left up to Brooke, she would have squandered away a few more minutes, but the Captain was a master of efficiency, and she resigned herself to telling the truth. "We need to have a discussion."

"We don't have to drive into town to have a discussion. We can discuss at the house."

No, they couldn't have this discussion at the house. The house was her home, and not having a lot of places to call home, she didn't want to ruin the memory of the first one she'd ever had. "Start the truck," she instructed, waiting patiently until the low rumble of the motor filled the cab.

The big black gates swung open, soon they were moving, the caliche gravel crunching under the tires.

"Did you talk to the lawyer?" he asked and there was worry in his voice. It pleased her that he might not be happy to say goodbye.

"No. But I talked to Gillian. I confessed the truth."

He glanced sideways, because the Captain was more cagey than Gillian, or perhaps he knew Brooke better than Gillian. "What truth did you tell her?"

For a man who valued honesty, he seemed tense, and maybe she should have spit things out more clearly, but that involved levels of personal growth that she had yet to obtain. "The one and only truth."

"You've got a lot of secrets up in the air, Brooke. Sometimes I have a hard time keeping track."

"Sarcasm is not necessary."

"What truth?" he asked.

Brooke gazed out the window, watching the oil wells that dotted the landscape as they passed. "I told her I couldn't afford the Inn, and I told her that Charlene Hart was a drinker and that I was working for you in order to generate income."

"Did you tell her anything else?" he asked.

She turned to study his profile this time, the quiet strength that she admired and envied, and the same quiet strength that made her want to cry. She wanted him to need her the way he needed air.

"You mean, did I tell her that I know you in the Biblical sense?" she said, some of her anger creeping into her voice.

He nodded. "That's the one."

"No."

"Smart."

"Gillian assumed things, though. However, in order to preserve your reputation, I denied it and told her that you were the perfect gentleman."

"I am the perfect gentleman."

"Who likes the sex."

"All men like the sex."

"Anyway, you're off the hook," she told him casually, because she didn't want him to invite her to stay out of a sense of responsibility or a guilty conscience. She wanted him to invite her to stay because he wanted her until he ached.

"What hook?"

Brooke smiled at him, as if it was the best sort of news. "Gillian and Austen are springing for a room at the Inn. Now I have a place to stay. I don't have to impose on you anymore."

MOST TIMES, Jason believed that the trips into town were too far and too long, but this time, the trip to Mrs. Kenley's house wasn't far or long enough.

He locked his hands on the wheel, shifted the gear into Park and concentrated on the one hundred and fifty pounds of metal in the bed of the truck instead of the forty kilotons of nuclear fission that just exploded in his gut.

Brooke looked at him, expected a response or, more precisely, an invitation, but Jason wasn't that guy and he escaped the suffocating cab, hopping up into the truck bed, focusing on what needed to be done.

Apparently it was a no-brainer for Brooke to believe that he wasn't that guy, she was already standing at the foot of the bed, laying the two-by-fours in place, waiting for him to slide the washing machine down the makeshift ramp. When had she gotten so efficient, when had she figured it all out? Uncomfortable with the idea that Brooke didn't need him anymore, Jason tugged at the bill of his cap, but the cap, the patch over his eye, not even the big fireball of the westerly sun wasn't enough to block her from his sight.

She met his eyes, and he could see so much there. All her dreams, all her pain, and there was a voice in his head that said, *Take her home, keep her forever.* But then she smiled at him, sad, smart and forgiving, and the voice in his head shut up.

"You need to train Dog to do this, Captain," she teased, smartly moving past the tension. "Otherwise he'll get fat and lazy."

Jason laughed, a hollow, rusty sound, and Mrs. Kenley waved from her front porch. Together, he and Brooke moved the washing machine up the porch and into the old laundry room on the back of the house.

"I appreciate the work, Captain. You always do such nice work." The woman laid a familiar hand on her machine and Jason understood. People bonded with their machines because machines were dependable and infallible. A machine could never disappoint.

Then she beamed at Brooke because people were always smiling at Brooke.

"I don't think we've met, honey. You're not Sonya unless you shrank about half a foot and dyed your hair." The old woman peered closer. "You're not Sonya, are you?"

Brooke chuckled, pushed at her hair and Jason could imagine the silk in his hands, until he jammed them in his pockets and he couldn't remember anything at all.

"No, I'm Brooke Hart. Yes, one of those Harts and, no, I don't have a criminal record."

"I like this one," Mrs. Kenley said to Jason. "You should keep her."

"This one? I thought I was the only one." Brooke

looked at him again, half teasing, mostly not, and his gaze shifted away.

"Should I make her jealous, Jason, or tell her the truth?"

No, he didn't want anyone to tell Brooke the truth. That was what he loved about her, that ability to not want to know the truth. Jason picked up the boards and the rollers and made for the door.

"Stump Tinkham said his afternoon soaps were breaking up, and he thought the antenna on the roof had gone wonky. I didn't say anything to him because you're always so busy, so I'm not going to say anything to you, either."

"I appreciate that, Mrs. Kenley. I won't stop by his house."

On the way home, Brooke was quiet until the big black gates yawned open to welcome him home. "You make these repair trips into town often?"

He managed a smile. "Nah. Not at all."

THEIR LAST DINNER TOGETHER was a quiet affair. More quiet than usual.

After Dog cleaned up, Brooke waited for the Captain to bury his head in some board or transistor or engine, but instead he brought out a large cardboard box.

"There are some things that you'll need, and some things I thought I would replace."

He deposited the package on the coffee table in front of her and took the chair opposite, waiting for her to open it.

Charlene Hart didn't believe in presents or surprises, at least not the good kind, so Brooke prepared herself to be disappointed. With shaky fingers, Brooke lifted the lid and then her breath caught.

Not disappointed here.

On top was a forest-green cashmere sweater. Not so practical in the Texas sun, but the wool was softer than anything she'd ever touched before. "It's lovely," she told him, lifting it out and holding it against her.

"Since I ruined the first one—"

Quickly she cut him off.

"This one is a lot nicer." She didn't know what a green cashmere sweater meant and she didn't want to think it meant anything, but the heart was a very hopeful thing. "Captain..."

Quickly he cut her off. "Go on. There's more," he said, and she focused her attention on the box. He was right, there was more.

A red sundress, complete with a matching red necklace. A new pair of shearling boots. Three pairs of jeans, a pencil skirt in charcoal gray and coordinating blouse in taupe. She'd never owned a pencil skirt before, and this one looked classy and sophisticated, and she thought she was going to love it. After that, her fingers dug through the box a little faster. Next was an old-fashioned cotton nightgown, with tiny flowers and delicate lace on the front.

It wasn't elegant and sophisticated. It was the most beautiful thing she'd ever owned. She met his eyes, dazed by the treasures in front of her. "This is too much."

"No. I ruined a lot of things for you. You're going to need all this. There's more."

More? Not sure what more entailed, she dug into the tissue paper, wondering if more meant a house key, a card, or a permanent toothbrush on the sink.

Instead, she pulled out a mobile phone and an envelope of cash. More truly sucked.

"You need a phone and the money's to get you started. Consider it an advance on your salary."

Salary. Oh, yes, that other thing she hadn't wanted to tell him. "Gillian found me a job at the court house. Filing."

"Filing is good. You'll be a good filer." He looked at her,

not sad at all, because in the end, the Captain was a practical person and Gillian had provided a practical solution, but Brooke was tired of being practical and strategic. Strategic thinking hadn't yielded the thing she wanted most of all.

"Captain," she started then his mouth was on hers and she couldn't breathe. His hands tangled in her hair, not practical, not sensible. No, this was perfect. The sort of impossible perfection that is so perfect that it hurts. Tears stung at her eyes, and the Captain lifted his head and swore. Gently, he wiped the moisture away, as if he didn't want to hurt her, but the tenderness was like a nail to her heart.

"I'm sorry," he apologized, as if a green cashmere sweater was a poor replacement for his heart, because it was. "I'll take the couch." Small words, painful words, and then he was pulling away. Her last night and he was robbing her of that, as well.

Brooke put a hand to his arm, asking for the last time. "Please?"

11

JASON FISTED HIS HAND in her hair and locked his mouth to hers. He closed his eyes, closed out the house, the world, ignoring everything but this. But her.

Strong hands dug into his shoulders, his neck. Not the timid hands that she'd used before. She stroked his hair, his scar, and the gentle touch hurt more than the IED ever had.

Needing to stop the pain, he lifted her in his arms, carrying her to bed. There was no moon, no stars. Here a man could hide himself in peace. With unsteady hands he undressed her, so careful not to rip, not to tear, not to ruin anything else. Brooke didn't know how fragile she was, but Jason did. He buried his face in the tangled silk of her hair, memorizing the feel of it against his cheek. His mouth whispered against her neck, lips moving with words he would never say. Blindly he found the sensitive spot beneath her right ear, felt her shiver in his arms, and he pulled her closer, wanting to make love to her in the way she deserved, but then her knee was sliding between his legs, rubbing his greedy cock and tortured balls, and he nearly...

No. Tonight was all about her.

"Captain," she whispered to him and he wished that he was. He wished that he was everything that she saw.

In the dark he filled her, completed her, adored her, and sometime before the dawn, when the night sky was done with black, she slipped from his bed and dressed.

THE SKY WAS GRAY, a tired, drizzling rain falling on the ground. Brooke stood on the front porch, her hands locked to the wooden railing until she made herself release it.

She had a new life waiting for her. The one she'd always wanted. A home. A family. Not perfect, but very, very real. Belonging. It felt good to belong. Comfortable, peaceful, safe.

Once she picked up the bag and box of her belongings, her feet descended the steps. One, two, three, four. The front walk was clear now, a tidy brick pathway that had been obscured from sight. She'd cleared a path to his doorway because...

No. The drops of rain fell in loud plops on the bricks, on her face, but the cool dampness suited her mood.

The entire yard was a lot neater now. Five sheds, newly painted and organized. A clipboard containing each inventory hung from a nail on the inside wall. He wouldn't lose things again. Yellow wildflowers poked up here and there among the grass. The Captain would call them weeds...

Her lips twitched into a sad semblance of a smile and this time when she scanned the yard, she noticed a sheet of plywood leaning against the side of the house. The rain would ruin the wood and make it unusable. She knew that now, and she grasped the rough edges, intending to move it out of the rain. It was a big one, six-by-six, she thought to herself, because she knew that now, too.

As she pulled, the wood revealed what had been hidden behind it.

Her fingers tightened on the plywood sheet because her knees had gone wobbly. There was the tub. Glistening ivory, with curly-cue legs and an elegant back. The rusted spots had been sand-blasted away, the fresh enamel was a smooth, pearly white. Now that the tub was exposed to the elements, the rain slid down the sides like a foolish girl's tears.

While she stood there, the rain picked up, turning into a stinging lash that whipped at her face, hitting the tub metal hard, but she couldn't move.

No one had ever done something like this for her... except the Captain.

One sob escaped her throat, only one because she had a new life waiting for her. A home. A job. A family.

A family. The Captain wasn't her family. He didn't want that.

No, this part of her life was done. With remarkably steady hands, she took the plywood and put it neatly back in place, and there was nothing left to prevent her from leaving. Brooke took one purposeful step with a new and improved mood and found the second step easier than the first. The lines and the curves of the path guided her, and then the steps came faster, because she knew she needed to do this fast, put him behind her before she stomped her self-respect into the mud.

The rain was falling in solid sheets now, her vision blurred completely, but she knew the way out. She had practiced this walk in her head, but she hadn't expected that her heart would weigh her down.

One last time she turned, and through the blur she could see the Captain on the porch, watching her go. Ruddy stubble lined his jaw, but there was no reason for him to shave now. His bare chest was riddled with puckered, silvery scars, long healed, long hardened. A pair of unfastened jeans clung to strong, capable thighs. But his bare feet weren't moving. His hands weren't beckoning her to stay because the Captain was strategic. One naked eye watched her, as stormy gray as the sky, and because Brooke's scars were fresh and raw, she stood frozen, waiting for the impossible.

The Captain stood tall, immovable. Brooked lifted her face to the rain.

This time she was smarter and stronger, and she wasn't so eager to fail. Outside those monstrous black gates was a life. *A future.* After keying in the combination, she waited impatiently for the gates to open and then loaded her things in the car. Before she drove away, she checked the mirror, safety first after all, and she could see the Captain still standing, locked away behind his black gates. She flipped on the windshield wipers, the rhythmic swish-swish like a knife slicing through her heart.

After the house disappeared from view, Brooke stopped the car at the side of the road. She cried and sobbed and swore, and by the time the rain had eased, she'd dried her eyes, repaired her makeup and was off to start her new life, leaving her heart and her tears behind her.

BROOKE SPENT MOST of Tuesday in the courthouse, learning the ins and outs of Sheriff Wanamaker's organizational system, of which there were none. Eventually, she shooed Gillian away, explaining that she needed to find her own method. Gillian seemed to understand. Promptly at five o'clock, Gillian appeared.

"You're ready for tomorrow?"

Tomorrow was the meeting with the lawyer. Gillian's face was drawn into a Mother Teresa look of concern and compassion, but Brooke wasn't fooled. This was about

Austen, the man she planned to marry. "I tried to call Austen yesterday, but he was tied up at the Capitol."

"He'll be at the old house in the morning. Meet him there."

Brooke looked into Gillian's eyes and knew this was it. No more stalling, no more avoidance. She could do this. The Captain believed in her, and it was time that Brooke did, as well.

"I'll be there."

"If you don't tell him, I will."

Brooke smiled. "You won't have to. I swear."

THE NEXT MORNING, she drove to the old house, and found her brother there, pulling down the last remains of the house and piling it in a long roll-off container. In the few short weeks since she'd lived in Tin Cup, she'd seen a different world than the one Charlene Hart had ever given her. Here, people did whatever needed to be done, fixed what was broken, and didn't whine about the process. Practical and simple. Brooke approved.

As she approached him, he was throwing in the last boards, and she jammed her hands in her jean pockets, waiting until Austen was done. "Thank you for what you're doing. For transferring over a part of the estate. You don't know what it means to me."

"It's the right thing to do. Legally, you're entitled. Before I sign the papers for the transfer, I wanted to talk to you. I wanted to get some things out in the open."

"Go ahead."

"I heard you were in charge of the ground-breaking ceremony for the train station?"

He winced. "That's something of an overstatement. I wrote a press release, and got JC here to speak. "

"Who's JC? What do you do for him?"

"Her."

"Oh."

He almost smiled. "Yeah. We get that a lot. She's running for governor next year, and I do her public relations, mainly. A lot of organizing events for the Masons and the PTA. A lot of writing, involving words like *leadership, growth* and *vision*. You want a bumper sticker?"

Brooke shot a sad glance at the Impala. "That wreck of a car might cost her the election."

He walked over, raised the hood and inspected the engine. "She's not too bad. A little body work. I could do a bit of tinkering under the hood. You'd be surprised with the difference. This car could be a thing of beauty with the proper amount of TLC."

"You're offering to fix it?" she asked.

He considered her for a moment. "Yeah. I could."

The generous offer was making it harder to confess her actual financial situation. "I might have misstated some things, and you might not like it."

"Don't know until you spit it out," he told her, pulling out a rag and wiping the grease from his hands.

"She wasn't very nice."

"Who?"

"Our mother."

"Sorry, sis. I wouldn't know."

She heard the sarcasm in his voice, and she spoke quickly before she lost her courage. "I photoshopped all those pictures on the wall in New York. The house wasn't even mine."

This time she had his full attention. "Go on."

"She liked to drink."

"No wonder she married Frank. It explains a lot." He laughed, but his eyes were shrewd. "Bet that really tweaked the preacher man, didn't it?"

Brooke stared at the ground. "I never had a preacher for a stepfather. I never had a stepfather."

"That was a lie, too? And the fiancé? Peter?"

"An acting student. I picked him up in a bar and paid him six hundred for the night."

For a long while Austen was quiet, and when he spoke, his voice wasn't nearly as mad as she had expected it would be. "Why didn't you just tell the truth?"

She looked at her car, looked out on the horizon, then looked at her brother with a sad smile. "I thought if I told you and Tyler that I was homeless, you two would get weird about it, but you both were weird about it anyway."

"We're not the family kind."

"I am."

"Sorry, sis."

She didn't believe his words. A man who was building a house for his bride? That was family. "I like Gillian. She's the family kind."

"Yeah."

"Do you want me to leave town? I can pack up my car and be on my way." Hopefully the car would make it.

"Is that what you want?"

She met his eyes. "No."

He waved a hand as if he didn't care. "Then don't."

"Are you ever going to stop being weird around me?"

Her brother shrugged.

"I need to belong somewhere," she said, by way of an explanation.

"And this is the place? There are a lot more glamorous locales."

"The people are nice."

"Except for Boolie Suggs at the *Tin Cup Gazette*. Don't cross her."

"Is that why the article said that Tyler was at the state pen?"

"Boolie likes to make things up. Now that I think of it, you might want to apply there. You two would really get along."

The words stung, and Brooke swallowed hard. "I should go." As she walked toward the car, Austen caught up with her.

"Brooke. Wait. I'm sorry. I figure once the wedding is over and this place is built, I won't be as irritable. Stay if you want, although to tell you the truth, if I didn't have something to keep me here, I'd be long gone. For the life of me, I just can't figure out why you'd want to stay here." He was staring at her ruefully. "Building a house in this little helltown isn't the smartest move I've made, but I'm here, too, which you could consider says something about both our smarts. I guess Tyler struck the motherlode when it comes to Hart brains."

"I bet you're really smart."

"Why do you think that?"

"Because Gillian is smart and I don't think she'd be marrying you otherwise."

He reached out and tweaked her nose, and no one had ever tweaked her nose before. It was a very brotherly thing to do and she found herself smiling. "Very perceptive, little sister. Maybe you inherited some brains, too. You're coming to the wedding?"

"My future sister-in-law would kill me if I didn't."

Austen laughed. "She's registered at Tallyrand's. I asked her, what's wrong with registering at Victoria's Secret, but no."

All the wariness was gone from her brother's eyes, and it occurred to Brooke that she should have told the truth a long time ago. The Captain was very smart that way.

Sometimes the truth wasn't so bad after all. "I think I'm going to like you."

"Buy her a black teddy for the wedding shower and I'll forgive you anything. And listen, before we talk to the lawyer, you should know something. There's some serious money on the table if we lease the mineral rights on the property. They're doing some seismic tests next week. It's not, oh-praise-jeezus-I'll-never-work-again money, but it'll keep you comfortable for a while."

Her brother had no idea how long Brooke could exist on very little funds. One man's comfortable is another woman's champagne dreams. "I like comfortable," she told him easily, as if her insides weren't screaming for joy. "You're going to the lawyer's?" she asked.

"Is it time?"

She held out her arm to her brother and smiled. "It's time."

THE LAWYER'S OFFICE was just as stuffy as Austen remembered, a dark, two-room place with a monstrous wooden desk, three leather chairs and four diplomas hanging from the wall. Six months ago he'd been here, walking away the not-so-proud owner of one half of the Hart house, appraised value of $837, one half of the Hart land, appraised at $7000 and one half of the mineral rights, value unknown. Little did he realize how such a small financial transaction could turn into an emotional goldmine.

Because of that one short trip back home, he'd found a new job and, best of all, found Gillian again. Today he was here to make things right for his sister. To pay her for her fair share of the inheritance and to sign over to her a third of the mineral rights.

"I prepared the paperwork, Austen. I think we have everything we need. You'll write a check to Miss Hart here for the financial value of the messuage." The lawyer paused, chuckling to himself. "Love that word. Just rolls off the tongue. That's lawyer-talk for house and land. Then we transfer one third of the mineral rights."

"Tyler signed his part, already? I tried to call yesterday but Edie—that's his girlfriend—said he was in surgery."

"I didn't need his signature. Tyler signed over his parcel to you already, Austen."

And they thought the lawyers knew it all? Ha. "I think you've made a mistake there, Hiram. He didn't say anything to me. Maybe you've got your last will and testaments confused."

The old lawyer pulled out a sheet of paper and slid it across the desk. "No mistake. All signed, sealed and delivered."

Austen studied the document, double-checked the signature and, God knows, it looked like that same illegible doctor's scrawl that Tyler used, but it couldn't be. He pushed the paper away.

"He would have told me," Austin insisted. Nobody knew his brother like he did. It wasn't that Tyler wasn't generous. It's just that he never thought of things like that. And since Austen didn't, either, it worked.

"He wanted to surprise you. A wedding present," the lawyer explained.

"Tyler doesn't like surprises."

"I bet Edie does," Brooke added in a quiet voice.

"If she made him do it…"

"Austen…" his sister began, smiling at him as if he were being a little slow. Now, normally Austen didn't mind that, but considering Brooke's recent disclosures, he didn't think that people in glass houses needed to be hurling stones. "She didn't make him do it."

"You know that for a fact?" he shot back, because he would feel more comfortable if duress had been involved.

"No, but call him. Ask him about Edie if it will make you feel better, but I think it's meant as a gift."

The lawyer coughed discreetly. "Dr. Hart was very insistent. I don't think there's any coercion here." He pulled out a business card and handed it to Brooke. "I believe Clayton Oakes is handling lease for the mineral rights. Nice fellow, does honest work, but watch the royalty rates. You can always negotiate a few points higher. I have his number written down, but call me if you think he's trying to low-ball you."

It was at that point that Austen stopped listening and waited for the world to resume it's normal, less dizzying rotation.

"Are you okay?" Brooke asked, sounding like a sister.

Austen slowly shook his head. "This isn't Tyler. Y'all don't know him. You know, the Harts, we're sort of 'all for no one' and 'no one for all.'"

Brooke laughed, a disbelieving laugh, as if they were a family. "Maybe you don't know him as well as you think. Maybe all for no one sucks. Why don't you call him? You should and, while you're gone, I'll have a chat with Hiram." Brooke looked happy, cheerful, as if this were a good thing.

Austen frowned, stared at the paper and then rose from the chair. "Yeah. Maybe I'll call."

Once outside, Austen pulled out his phone and tapped Tyler's number on the touch screen, and then quit. What was he supposed to say to his brother? Thanks? What the hell are you doing?

A wedding present? Sure, he expected his brother to give him something. A silver tankard with the date engraved on it. Maybe some fancy plates or crystal. But this?

There were lines here that weren't usually crossed. On

Tyler's birthday, Austen sent a card and a gift certificate to a nice restaurant, usually a steak house, because they'd never had a lot of expensive meat growing up. At Christmas, Tyler called and told him "Merry Christmas," and then sent him a sweater. Always cashmere. Usually blue.

As for Thanksgiving, that was a holiday usually spent solo. There were strict rules in the Hart family, and here went Tyler, breaking a rule—and Tyler was not, as a rule, a rule-breaker.

Austen sat on the curb and stared down the main street of Tin Cup, noticing the friendly waves in his direction and the way it all felt so…*good*.

So when had this hell turned into home? Was it when Dot started sliding him extra bacon with his breakfast at the diner? Or when Gillian's parents had told him and Gillian to take the Hart land and build a new and better house on it, something for Austen and Gillian, and the grandkids when they came?

So many bad memoires of Tin Cup, Texas, but not anymore. Now, the memories were coming up good—Brooke Hart included. Still contemplating this new, contented sort of feeling, Austen hit Tyler's number on the phone and waited, waited.

Finally, it was no surprise when he reached his brother's voice mail.

"Ty? It's Austen. Your brother. The lawyer told me what you did. Thanks. Say, Edie didn't put a gun to your head, did she? Nah, I'm sure she didn't, but it's nice what you did. You didn't have to. I mean, I know you're not suffering for cash or anything, but, dude…it's nice. Thanks."

After that, he hung up, laughed at his own foolishness, and then called Tyler's number again, waiting patiently for the beep.

"And one more thing. I know you're going to be here

for the wedding, but could you and Edie stay on through Thanksgiving? We should do that, don't you think? We'll get some turkey and beer...and watch football. Gillian will love it. What do you think? I'd like to have you down here, bro. It'd be nice. We're family."

Austen hung up and smiled.

Family, what a concept.

Then he called his brother's voice mail again.

"I promise this is the last message, but I talked to Brooke this morning. Lots of crazy shit to tell you, bro. You wouldn't believe it. She was lying her ass off about the stepdad, the house, getting married and Charlene taking her on all those trips." He laughed, and it was a good laugh. "Yeah, she's definitely one of us. I think I'm going to like her."

THE LAWYER SHUFFLED his papers, coughing in that way people have when they're annoyed, but don't want the world to know they're annoyed, but of course, the world knows anyway. "I'm sorry I missed you last week. If I had known you had your birth certificate, I would have let Austen proceed with the paperwork. You can't be too cautious these days. I hope you understand."

Brooke understood only too well. "How is your father?"

"Better, thank you for asking. He's not a good patient, and likes to have someone to listen to his complaints. I'm sorry that it took longer than I thought. Did Mr. Kincaid give you my message?"

Brooke lifted her head. "No, he didn't say a word."

"I called the number you left for me."

"The Captain is a very busy man. I'm sure it slipped his mind," she assured Mr. Hadley, knowing very well it hadn't slipped the Captain's mind.

"Not that it matters," the lawyer droned on. "Mr. Oakes

will need your signature on the mineral rights lease, assuming the signing bonus and royalty rates are agreeable. Remember what I said, don't let Clayton low-ball you. It's a tidy sum, and I bet a little extra revenue will come in handy. First, the train station, now some new oil and gas work. The times, they are a-changing, don't you agree?"

Brooke blinked, recognized the man was waiting for an answer and nodded stupidly. Why hadn't the Captain said something? She told herself not to read anything into it. Most likely he'd forgotten, or he hadn't thought it was important, or maybe there were a million other reasons that meant nothing at all.

Still, after transfer of the mineral rights was done and Austen's check was folded neatly in her pocket, Brooke sprang from her seat with an extra happy bounce.

No, she didn't want to read anything into it, but maybe the times were a-changing after all.

Jason was outside, removing nails from some old railroad ties, when he heard a ringing noise coming from the house. The phone.

Jason's first thought was that Brooke was calling, that her car had broken down, that she'd lost her job, that she needed something. Him. But then he lifted his head, checked the desolate landscape and realized that mirages existed not only in the desert, but also in brain-dead men's imaginations, too.

However, he laid down the nail puller and headed for the house, his stride a little faster than it should be for a man who didn't believe in the power of his imagination.

"Kincaid," he answered, keeping his voice curt and not regretful at all.

"Jason, it's George."

As Jason listened to his brother, a chunk of bile rose in

his throat. He tasted scrambled eggs and felt the hot sun grow cold. Quiet and alone, he sank down to the couch and stared until the vision in his one good eye grew blessedly dim.

THERE WAS A MINDLESS COMFORT in copying and filing that Brooke needed at the moment. Leaving the Captain had left an emptiness inside her just as she was starting to learn exactly what *together* could mean. Sometimes when she walked along the friendly streets of town, she felt so very alone, looking at a world that she'd always wanted to be a part of, and yet feeling as if she'd never belong.

Maybe some people were born with the ability to blend in, whatever their surroundings, but not Brooke. Not yet, but hopefully she could learn.

She suspected that Gillian had dug up some busy-work for her that had been ignored, and it seemed that all around her, people were going out of their way to help Brooke get on her feet. Hiram had told her about a small apartment that would be vacant before the end of the year, and the rent was cheap, even by Brooke's standards. Gillian's mother had been bringing small casseroles by the Spotlight Inn so that Brooke wouldn't have to go into town to eat if she didn't feel like it. And best of all was Austen. He'd changed the oil and transmission fluid on the Impala. Helped her pick out a new rear tire—apparently the old one was on its last treads. He was starting to feel like an older brother.

Next door in Gillian's office, Brooke could hear her arguing on the phone in that butter-melts-in-her-mouth fashion that Gillian had. In the end, Gillian usually got what she wanted, but apparently not this time.

The normally coolheaded woman flung open her office door and screamed.

Politely Brooke laid the files on the floor. "Is there a problem?"

"This wedding is going to kill me. It's supposed to be the happiest day of my life, but do you think anybody gives a rat's patootie? Heck, no. It's just, 'I don't think we can get lilacs in November, Gillian.' Can you believe it? This is America. They can get whatever the heck they want, and who cares if it's November? Ask me if I care if it's a free-range lilac or a genetically pure lilac. I just want my lilac. Do you think I'm crazy?"

Brooke decided it wouldn't be the best time to laugh. "You're not being crazy. Maybe I can help."

Gillian raised a brow. "You can get lilacs for me?"

"No, but I bet I can get the florist to work a little harder."

Gillian looked doubtful and, yes, Brooke couldn't blame her for that, but frankly, people needed to stop underestimating what Brooke was capable of, and the best route to do that was for Brooke to step up to the plate and throw a touchdown, or something like that.

"You don't mind?" She crossed her eyes and still looked gorgeous. "I'd be soooo grateful."

"Not a problem. Let me give it a shot." Brooke stood, rolled her shoulders and prepared for battle. "I'll get you the lilacs. I swear."

WHAT IN CARNATION was a tiny shop full of flowers and stuffed teddy bears, and one very busy florist, Luna Chavez, who bustled back and forth, but had a calming, zen sort of smile.

"I'm acting for Gillian Wanamaker. She doesn't know I'm here, but when I left the courthouse, she was in tears, and I had to do something."

"Tears?" Luna put down her scissors, concern in her eyes.

Brooke hesitated, then nodded. "You think a strong woman like that would never cry, don't you?"

"I felt so bad, but there is nothing I can do," Luna explained, holding her hands up innocently.

"No way to get the lilacs in?"

"I tried very hard, but they're not in season, and the plants will not grow whenever we want. It is nature's way."

Brooke exhaled, deeply, sadly. "It's too bad that nature has to be so cruel. First her mother... Now this." Slowly, head down, Brooke moved toward the door.

"Her mother?"

Brooke turned and shrugged as if the weight of the world was a heavy, heavy thing. "Don't worry. I'm sure she'll be fine."

Now Luna was clearly alarmed. "Wait! Is there something wrong with Modine?"

"Maybe I shouldn't say anything, maybe I'm butting in where I shouldn't, but I love Gillian like she's my own sister, and she's just too proud to tell people what's really going on. The Wanamakers are very proud people, but of course, I'm not telling you anything that you don't know."

"Has Modine seen a doctor?"

"It's all very hush-hush. I'm sure it's nothing. But the waiting is awful. It would mean so much to Gillian if she could make everything as easy as possible. Austen would be here to handle a lot of these details, but he's at the Capitol today, planning for that breaking-ground ceremony for the new rail line, and Gillian was just ready to give up, and she never gives up, which tells you how bad it is...."

"I didn't know."

Brooke shot her a calming, very zen smile. "I know. Don't worry about it. It's nature's way."

This time, Luna was not so accepting of the adage. Give these people a crisis and who knew what they could do? "I could call my wholesalers in Houston, but it's a long way, and they'll charge an arm and a leg for delivery."

"I'm sure that Gillian will pay whatever is necessary," Brooke assured the woman, not that it was going to come to that. She poked at the nearest teddy bear and managed a sad smile. "Not that she's having an easy time of it, you understand, having to support her mother and father, God bless them. I can't believe that in this day and age, folks can be so generous around here...." Brooke laughed. "But of course you know that."

"I would never charge her the full price for the delivery. Miss Gillian is very nice."

"Of course not. I can see how much her family means to you, and you've got such a sweet, kind-hearted face..." Brooke hugged the teddy bear to her chest and smiled.

"Let me get the wholesaler on the phone. Dan is the manager and he likes me. They shipped me a lot of limp roses last month, and he offered to give me a break on another delivery. It's time I took him up on that offer."

Brooke nodded politely. "I'll wait."

Yes, whenever there was a crisis afoot, people could work miracles. She'd have to remember that in the future.

While Luna disappeared, Brooke picked through the cards on display, eyeing the brightly colored planters, and sighing at the rose bouquet in the window. The roses were plastic, since real flowers would never last, but even plastic flowers were better than none.

Behind the glass counter, there was a trio of plants and flowers sitting in a box, waiting to be delivered, and Brooke decided that nobody would care if she poked through them to see who was getting what. Out of the corner of her eye she checked to make sure that the coast was clear and bent to look at the arrangements. Henry Hinkle was sending a bouquet of daisies to his wife for their anniversary. Brooke smiled and made a note to herself to stop by the grocery later and wish them well.

Apparently the librarian was in the hospital—Brooke would have to ask Gillian about that—although it probably wasn't serious because the pot of delicate flowers was topped with smiley-faced balloons, and who sent balloons if it was serious? No, serious was the somber little plant in the corner with the maroon satin bow. The wooden container was square and plain. Square and plain meant serious. One Valentine's Day, Brooke was temping at a florist's, mainly to get bus fare out of Cleveland, and she knew a little. No, the little plant didn't bode well for someone.

Carefully she opened the card.

Jason, I'm very sorry for your loss. Your Father was
a very special man. Love, Sonya.

Jason? The Captain?
No....
Suddenly not caring so much about balloons and blooms, Brooke grabbed the delivery sheet and checked the last name to see if there was more than one Jason in Tin Cup, Texas, population two thousand one hundred and forty-seven.

Jason Kincaid.
Oh, God.
Brooke peeked into the back of the shop, but Luna was still on the phone.

The lilacs would have to wait.

12

JASON OPENED THE DOOR and found Brooke on his doorstep, sympathy in her eyes.

"I'm sorry."

"I'm fine," he answered, not inviting her in because he didn't need sympathy.

"Can I come in?"

"No. I'm not very good company."

"You were never good company." Then Ms. Brooke Hart, who only got pushy at the worst possible times, brushed past him to make her way inside.

Once there, she scanned the room, noting the stack of dishes in the sink, Dog unplugged in the corner, and the half finished bottle of Jack Daniels sitting next to a computer terminal. He didn't want her to see this, didn't want her to see him like this, but he wasn't completely blind, and unfortunately, neither was she.

Tired and hung over, he rubbed at his face, the stubble like a wire brush scratching his hands. He frowned, trying to remember when he'd last shaved.

Brooke came to stand in front of him, put a hand on his arm. "Captain."

"I was a Staff Sergeant. Not a captain."

Instead of arguing, she took his arm and led him out to the porch, the midmorning sun bright in his eyes.

"You look like hell," she stated, no sympathy in her voice at all. With more force than he deserved, she pushed him down on the polished red leather bench seat.

"I've missed you, too," he said, wishing for sunglasses, anything to block out the light, because his head felt as if it had been detonated—never a good sign.

"Do you have a headache?" she yelled, speaking louder than necessary.

"I'm not deaf."

"Do you need aspirin?" she bellowed into his ear.

He started to tell her to go away, but although Jason might be knuckle-headed about some things, he'd never been a liar. "Yes."

"Do you have aspirin?" she asked in a more humane voice now that she had broken his will.

"In the cabinet," he answered, and once again Brooke was leaving. When she returned, she held out two pills and a glass of water.

Not wanting to look too eager, Jason swallowed the pills and the water. Brooke sat next to him on the swing and waited quietly for the hammering in his head to stop.

Fifteen minutes had passed when Brooke reached for his hand, taking advantage of his weakened state. He let her.

Slowly the explosions in his head began to ease and the sun rose higher, losing its laser sights on him.

"Thank you," he told her.

"You could have called me."

No, he couldn't. Calling her implied that he needed her. Calling her implied that he had lain awake with a hole in his gut. No, calling her was out.

Cowardly avoiding that conversation, Jason stayed silent.

"Tell me about him," she asked.

"Not much to tell," he answered, because he didn't know how to talk about that, either.

"I never knew my father, and I'm not complaining because I think it's a good thing I never met Frank Hart, but I like the idea of a father. Tell me about yours."

Her quiet words made him feel like an ass. On the life scale of bad things to happen to people, Brooke outranked him, but very few people would ever guess that. It was a humbling experience to be outmanned by a girl.

To make her happy he began to talk. He told her about the furniture that his father had built, the set of pirate-ship bunkbeds that he'd given Jason on his seventh birthday. Jason told her about his first car, a 1947 army jeep that he and his father had rebuilt. There were so many things to tell her, and the words tumbled out. About the three-bedroom house in Maryland, and the arguments he'd had when Sara hogged the bathroom. He told her about the model rockets he'd built with his father, specifically the Little John missile, the most powerful rocket ever engineered for hobby purposes, especially with the retrofitted nitrous-oxide boosters. Everything had been great until it scared the neighbor's cat and Mrs. Chapman threatened to call the police. Jason's father promised to patch the cracks in her dilapidated sidewalk if she wouldn't.

For a long time he talked and Brooke listened, soaking up his life like a sponge. It was late in the afternoon, when the sun was shimmering on the grass and the air was starting to cool, that his voice grew rusty from use.

"When's the funeral?" she asked.

"Day after tomorrow. They delayed it until the weekend so that David could fly in from California."

"You're not going, are you?"

He didn't like the way she said it, like there was something wrong with his decision.

"What's the point of a funeral? People are dead, they're dead."

"Did you ever think your family might need you?"

"No."

"You're making some very poor decisions that you're going to regret for the rest of your life. You're too smart to be so stupid." Then she slipped her hand from his and stood. "I have to go. Gillian needs lilacs and the florist is going to close soon. You should fly to Maryland, Captain."

She'd never looked at him like that before, clear-eyed, not missing a thing.

Then she turned and left him again, and he noticed that she didn't hesitate this time and it hurt. Wanting to make her turn around, he called after her.

"I'm a Staff Sergeant, not a captain."

Brooke didn't turn around, didn't look at him. Instead she lifted her hand in an unladylike gesture that was beneath her.

It was nothing less than he deserved.

HIS BROTHER GREETED HIM on the doorstep, looking older, the coppery-brown hair thinned near the top. "I'm glad you came."

"It's family," Jason told him. "It's what you do."

Then his brother clasped him on the shoulder. "Sara's not taking this very well," he said, and Jason heard the crack in his voice because George had always been the soft one.

Jason nodded once, and George pulled him into a hug, and when Jason smelled the ghost of his father's aftershave, his eyes filled with tears, and silently the two brothers stood in the doorway and wept.

THE GROUND BREAKING for the train station was the third Thursday in October, and Jason hadn't meant to go, but he ended up doing his grocery shopping that day, and maybe he'd dressed a little nicer than usual to go grocery shopping, but he thought that as a citizen of the community, it made sense to show some civic pride.

The land had already been cleared, red construction flags tagging the perimeter. Off to the left side, two rows of chairs were set aside for dignitaries, and the Tin Cup High School band was playing Dr. Who.

Idly he scanned the crowd, looking for familiar faces until he found Brooke's. She was standing next to her brother, in the chic-chic skirt and blouse that he'd bought for her, and she looked exactly like he knew she would. The crowd was filled with overalls and jeans, but Brooke stood apart from the others, poised and polished, her dark hair twisted up in a bun. Finally she had come into her own, dumped the little-lost-Brooke look, because it was obvious even to a one-eyed man that she'd found her home at last.

The old mayor hobbled out first, rambling about cattle drives and whorehouses until Gillian interrupted his speech and brought JC Travis up to the stage. It was a smart move for the woman who had rescued the town, kicking off her campaign for governor here. She spoke of the future she envisioned, how they needed to look forward and be ready for a new town, a new state, a new world. Her words were full of inspiration and hope, and the crowd stayed stone-cold silent, lapping it up, because a small town needed to believe in itself. Then she and the mayor picked up their shovels and dug into the dirt. As actual work went, it didn't amount to much, but all around Jason, people whistled and cheered.

It was then that Brooke noticed him. She nodded warily and he nodded back, waiting for her to come to his side. Ten long minutes passed before he figured out that she wasn't going to come to him, and he told himself he should ditch the whole thing and go home. Then she met his eyes and his head started swimming, and he found himself walking over—just to say hello and to see how she was. It was a matter of civic pride.

"How are you?" she asked, poised and untouchable, even her freckles were hidden underneath her makeup, and Jason felt an irrational urge to wipe it all away.

But, no.

"I'm good," he answered, completely rational. "I went to the funeral," he added, surprised that he was telling her, but pleased with her smile.

"I'm glad."

"You were right," he added, because he owed her that.

"I know."

"How's things with your brother?"

She smiled up at Jason, looking not so untouchable, and he jammed his hands into his pockets. "He's a goofball. I didn't know that."

"A lot of men are. Don't hold it against him."

She giggled, an unrestrained gurgle of laughter and he realized how much he missed that sound.

"Are you still at the Inn?"

"For now. At the end of the year, I'm renting a room from Doc Emerson."

Jason frowned because she belonged in a real house, a real home. "The Doc's got a bad track record on maintenance. I overhauled his AC unit two years ago, and it was a wreck. You should have your own home."

"I'm saving up for my own place. Something small, and close to Austen and Gillian's new place. With room for a garden. I've always wanted a garden. And now I have a nest egg. I've never had a nest egg before. And maybe I'll have a bigger nest egg, we're not sure."

She was talking fast and when she caught on to what she was doing, he saw the flush on her face. Something sharp and painful squeezed in his chest because even in pencil skirt and heels, she was still the woman he loved.

"Why are you not sure?"

"We're leasing the mineral rights on the property, and the signing check is awfully sweet, but Austen negotiated an extra deal. He said the oil companies are all a bunch of sharks, and you have to be careful. So if the seismic tests go well, and it looks like we have oil underground, they'll kick in a bonus."

Once again something sharp and painful squeezed in his chest because she was going to get her nest egg. She was going to get her house. Her garden. Her life. And that was his signal to leave. Jason managed a tight smile. "Don't worry. I've got a good feeling about that. I bet you get everything you want."

TWO WEEKS LATER, Brooke's life had settled into a regular routine. Her days were spent at the courthouse, at night she went over to help Gillian with the wedding preparations, and then finally, when exhaustion set in, she would drive to the Inn and fall into bed, hoping for a long, peaceful sleep.

The sleep was long in coming, and sometimes it was peaceful with the most marvelous dreams where the Captain was dreaming next to her. On those mornings, she woke up with a smile on her face—until she realized she was alone. It was at that moment that she plastered a smile on her face, opened the curtains, took a hot shower and told herself that everything would be fine.

When she walked into the courthouse, Mindy and Gillian were waiting for her. Mindy had her car keys in hand, sunglasses on her head, and Gillian was holding up *People* magazine and waving an envelope.

"I'm pleased to report that no longer will they say that your check is in the mail. Mr. Hadley dropped this off a half hour ago."

"What is this?"

"Bonus check. Gotta love the oil business."

Slowly Brooke pulled the check out of the envelope and gazed in awe, counting and recounting the zeroes in case there had been a mistake. No mistake.

"Come on. We're headed to the Canyon Lake spa for a little R&R. We deserve it. And as you can now afford it, and as my almost-sister, you get to come along and listen to me fret. They serve wine with the mud baths, so that'll dull the sound of my whining. I promise."

"I have to work," Brooke began, because she had heard of these things called spas, but she'd never seen one, been at one, and... She glanced down at the check in her hands.

"Darling, one thing you have got to learn if you want to fit in here—and you do want to fit in, don't you?"

Mindy bobbed her head. "Of course she does."

Gillian took Brooke's arm and began leading her out the door. "You have to learn to relax and have fun, let down your hair a little."

"Speaking of hair, can I get a cut? Junior's started pulling mine, and that kid has got some power in his grip. Takes after his daddy, I think."

Gillian looked at Brooke, pushed her sunglasses low on her nose. "What do you say?"

Once again Brooke looked at the check. This was real. "Oh, my God. I'm in."

BROOKE HAD NEVER BEEN wrapped in mud before. She'd never worn cucumbers on her eyes. She'd never had her hair blown out and, most of all, she'd never looked so gorgeous…and the Captain would never see.

They were riding in Mindy's car, hitting the interstate and heading for home. Mindy and Gillian were in the front seat chattering about the wedding until Gillian noticed that Brooke wasn't saying much at all. "For a woman who's just been manicured and fluffed, you're looking mighty sad. If you're going to be sad, I have failed in my duty as a positive influence."

Mindy snickered. "You are no one's positive influence, Gillian. You just like to think that."

"Hush up, former BFF. Don't disillusion the girl before she's gotten a chance to love my good side."

"It's been a lot of fun," Brooke said, because it had been fun, until it hadn't.

"Then why are we not smiling?"

"I don't know."

"She's just got a case of the sads, Gillian. Let her be."

"Is that all?" Gillian asked, lifting her sunglasses and studying Brooke's face.

Brooke nodded, but Gillian didn't seem convinced. "Things will get better. I promise. Make some new friends. Hey, you show up at Smitty's looking like that and it'll start a riot."

"That would be nice," Brooke told her, with absolutely no enthusiasm.

"You've got some hurts that need healing?"

Brooke shook her head because Gillian had enough to worry about.

Gillian reached over to the backseat and patted her knee, an encouraging smile on her face. "Don't worry, honey. It'll go away."

"You're sure?" asked Brooke.

"Depends on how bad you got it," Mindy added,

glancing over her shoulder. "A woman can crush on a guy or lust for a guy, and that sort of hurt, that goes away. Sure, it smacks on the ego, but eventually it disappears."

Brooke wasn't sure that it would disappear. There wasn't another man in the world with a heart like the Captain's, and there was no other heart that she wanted more.

Noticing Brooke's doubtful expression, Gillian's perky smiled faded. "It's the real stuff that hangs on and stings like a mother. Shopping and wine, they'll make you feel better, but then the ship sinks and you're floating alone on a piece of ice in the ocean, and all around you, everybody else has found a lifeboat, but not you, no, you're in the water, freezing and dying, and somewhere in the distance, Celine Dion starts to sing. That, my friend, is the misery of love."

It was dark when Mindy's car whizzed passed the Welcome to Tin Cup, Texas, sign and Brooke felt as warm and well pampered as a hand-rolled limp noodle. Her skin had never glowed like a pearl, her hair had never been so glossy and thick and the sleek black designer dress that she'd bought made her look like a million dollars. She'd never paid that much money for a dress before, but Gillian had told her that she needed to splurge every now and then, and Brooke had talked the price down another twenty percent because the prices were highway robbery. In the end, Brooke had waltzed out of the store, turning heads as she passed.

This was a new experience, feeling as if she'd been reborn. Brooke didn't usually like inviting male attention because it never ended well, but this was her new life, her new future, Gillian and Mindy encouraging her every high-heeled step of the way. All evening Brooke had watched and learned, and by the time the dinner at the fancy Austin restaurant was done, the waiter was eating out of Brooke's hand, too.

It was a shame to waste all that effort on Delores at the Spotlight Inn, so after Gillian dropped her off, Brooke climbed into the beat-up Impala. For a second she hesitated, until she examined her own reflection in the mirror, the confident smile, the million-dollar hair. She shook out her expensive do and decided that there was no better time to show up at the Captain's door and show him who Brooke Hart really was.

He greeted her at the door, and she was pleased to see the flash of heat in his gaze. "You look nice."

"Thank you. Gillian and Mindy took me to Austin for a day of beauty, and I wanted to show off. Can I come in?"

The heat dimmed, but he nodded and stepped aside.

The front room looked a lot better this time. The dishes were put away, Dog was idling in the corner, and there was a bowl of fruit on the kitchen table.

"I like the hair."

She made a great show of swishing it around, just like in the shampoo commercials. "It's great. They put a special treatment on it, I thought it felt like grease, but it smelled a whole lot better. And here," she said, stepping close and holding up a strand. "You should feel."

The Captain took the strand, and dropped it as if it burned. "Nice."

"Do you mind if I sit down?" she asked, and before he could answer, she seated herself on the couch, legs crossed oh-so-seductively so that he could notice that the skin of her legs was as smooth and buffed as the rest of her.

His good eye rested on her legs and then rose up to her face and, sadly, he knew exactly what she was doing. Brooke crossed her arms over her chest, not defensively, not at all.

"Make yourself at home," he offered, taking the chair opposite her and she studied him, noticing the changes. He was shaving, a tiny nick under his scar, and his hair had been cut. Some of the scruffiness was gone, and she realized that she wasn't the only one who had gotten some polish.

"What are you working on now?" she asked, a poor attempt at conversation because, despite her newfound confidence, her man-handling skills weren't nearly as good as she needed them to be.

"Automatic garage-door monitor for Ernestine Landry. She forgets and leaves the door up at night. I put up a signal in her bedroom. Green is shut. Red is up."

"I'm glad you're getting out more."

"Not that much."

"Still." She picked up the decorative throw pillow on the sofa and smiled. "It's nice. The place looks...friendlier."

"Thank you."

She sat there for a few more minutes, acknowledging that her man-handling skills were crap, and finally she rose and smoothed the dress's tight skirt over her thighs. "I should go."

He didn't argue with her and showed her to the door, but then Brooke faced him because she'd never felt so mouth-wateringly gorgeous, so ready to live a grand life. He wasn't supposed to be able to ignore her. Not the Captain.

Like always, she reached up and pressed a kiss on his cheek, and then his arms were around her, and he was kissing her urgently. With a laugh, she tangled her hands in his hair, hearing a low hungry growl in this throat. His hands slid under her dress, tugging the material up because it had been too long, and tonight she wanted him to fill her.

Like always, her legs parted, and she didn't think he

noticed that she was smooth and buffed. Like always, his hands gripped her, cupping her to him and she smiled against his lips, her thighs cradling his heavy cock, feeling a surge of desire filling her sex, a surge of emotion filling her heart. For Brooke, this was home. He was the only home she had.

She raised her head, opened her eyes, and her fingers moved to the buttons down the front of her dress. "I want to do this for you."

The Captain stepped back, his breathing ragged, his erection straining against his jeans, his face flushed with everything he wouldn't admit, but it was the steady look in his eye that defeated her. It didn't matter how pretty she was, or how buffed she was, or how much he wanted her. For the Captain, it would never be enough.

"Brooke," he began and quickly she shook her head.

"No. This is no more than what was always between us," she promised. She slid the top buttons open, revealing the satin bra beneath. "I bought it for you. I wanted to see your face when I showed it to you."

It wasn't lust on his face, but caution.

"Don't do this," he warned, but she didn't listen, because she didn't want to listen. She wanted the sparks and the fire and all those things that normal people were supposed to have. She wanted his mouth on hers, she wanted to feel him hard between her thighs. What the hell was wrong with that?

She made a move to slide off her bra, but he stopped her with strong hands, unshakable hands.

"Stop. You have no idea how beautiful you are. How perfect you look in silk and pearls."

She could hear the pain in his voice, but it didn't matter.

Not when he was throwing her away. Not when he was throwing them away. "I did it for you," she pleaded.

"No. You did this for you. You need to know who you are, what you're capable of. You have a shot, Brooke. Don't waste it on me."

"Waste it?" she said, her voice loud in the quiet room. "This is right. We are right. I love you, Captain."

"Jason. My name is Jason. You should learn it. You should use it."

Why couldn't he see? "You don't understand. You will always be a captain to me. My Captain."

Sadly he shook his head. "You just started getting your training wheels, Brooke. You're finally where you want to be. Live that life. You deserve that life."

"I deserve more. The bravest. The most noble, the most honorable. The best of them all."

"Then go find him."

They weren't the words that she'd dreamed of, and in that instant she hated the expensive bra and the smooth, buffed skin and everything that she had done. She wanted to hurt him, wanted to throw the words back in his face, but instead she pulled down her black skirt, buttoned up the luxurious silk of her dress and turned to him because she would not lie. No more lies. He'd taught her that. He thought she needed to search for the best and the bravest?

She looked at him, eyes filled with tears, her voice filled with anger.

"He's already here."

JASON STOOD IN THE DOORWAY for a long, long time thinking that she'd come back, but eventually the darkness swallowed her up and he could hear the fading sound of the rattling cylinders of her engine and he knew she wasn't coming back.

He closed the door, turned out the lights, and Dog whirled next to him, bright LED eyes that never saw, never felt, never loved. It was the cold comfort that he'd always craved.

For the first time, though, cold comfort wasn't enough.

13

FORTUNATELY FOR BROOKE, the days before the wedding passed quickly. During the days, she would work at the courthouse, and at night she stayed at Gillian's house until late, doing whatever was necessary to make sure that her future sister-in-law stayed sane. Brooke had never imagined the stress involved in planning a wedding, and each day she watched Gillian decline into what Austen termed "Bridezilla."

Sometimes Austen and Gillian would go for a drive, and Brooke would stay behind with Gillian's parents, doing what she could to help, and puzzling over the odd dynamics of this family thing.

It wasn't exactly what she expected. There were arguments and times that she'd rush off to her room at the Inn, soaking in the tiny bathtub, crying at the late-night movies on TV. Sometimes it didn't matter if the movie was sad or not. Sometimes she just cried.

She didn't see the Captain in town, not that she thought she would, but sometimes she would sit in Dot's diner for breakfast and hear someone mention his name.

On the Tuesday before the wedding, Tyler and Edie arrived. Tyler was quiet and somber, choosing to sit back and listen, letting Austen or Edie dominate the conversation. Sometimes he would peer at Brooke curiously, and she wasn't sure if he approved of her or not.

Friday night, before he and Austen took off for a bachelor party, which Gillian insisted that she didn't want to know anything about, Brooke gathered her courage and decided to approach Tyler just like a sister would, which basically meant cornering him in the kitchen before he could run.

"You look like her," she told him. "You have her nose."

He stared impassively. "I never noticed."

"She was passed out a lot. I studied her a lot."

"I'm sorry."

"Don't be," she told him. In many ways it had been worse for them. Sometimes unconscious and passed out was better. "I like Austen."

"He's easy to like," Tyler stated, his voice flat and calm. Maybe it was the doctor thing, or maybe he just didn't like her.

Brooke tried again. "The day in the lawyer's office. You really got to him. He wasn't expecting that."

At last, success. Tyler's mouth slowly drew up in a smile. "Good."

"I haven't had a lot of practice with this."

"What?"

"Families. I might say something weird, or do the wrong thing, but it's only because I don't know exactly what to do. I might make a lot of mistakes, but don't give up on me. You and Austen are all I have."

He looked surprised and almost pleased, but before he could say anything, Austen grabbed him by the arm, pushing a cowboy hat on Tyler's head. "There. Now you look like a fake Texan. People will buy you extra shots, just for the hat alone."

Tyler was eyeing his brother, but Brooke knew that his words were for her. "I'm in for the long haul, whatever it takes."

IT WAS FIVE DAYS BEFORE the wedding, past 1:00 a.m., and Gillian was in her living room, stuffing candy hearts into red velvet pouches.

"Candy hearts?"' asked Austen, coming to sit next to her, and thankfully, not snickering too loud.

"I saw it in *Modern Bride,*" she explained, which she liked as an answer because people only nodded, as if no more words were required.

"You can't sleep?" asked her future husband, guessing correctly because he saw more than most.

She shoved the piles of pouches aside and threw herself into his arms. "Nerves. Sexual frustration. I think I've had too much caffeine."

"I can solve one of those problems."

She drew back, drawing strength from the easy confidence in his eyes. "I want it to be perfect."

"I thought it was always perfect," he teased.

"The wedding, not the sex."

"Okay. I can live with that."

She glared at him, signaling that this was important.

"The wedding's going to be perfect," he assured her.

She picked up a candy heart and popped it in her mouth, until she remembered that she hadn't run today and she couldn't afford the calories. "I'm worried."

"We could always elope," he said as he pulled her into his arms, squeezing tight, and she stayed there a moment, temporarily considering the idea. "It's going to be great," he promised.

"It's Jason."

"Kincaid? Why are we talking about Jason Kincaid?" he asked, his hand gently stroking her hair.

"He has to be at the wedding. She loves him. He loves her, but he's being very stubborn."

His hand stilled. "Who loves him?"

"Your sister. Can't you tell?"

"Most likely you're just so much in love that you're seeing it everywhere."

"Don't be a tool," she warned, because after four cups of coffee, teasing would not be tolerated.

"Only your tool, darling. Only yours."

She lifted her head, giving him the full force of the Gillian Wanamaker gaze. "You'll get him there?"

"I'm no miracle worker." He looked doubtful, and it tugged at her heart that he still didn't know how many miracles he'd performed.

Gently she kissed him, feeling the same jump in her pulse as though she were sixteen all over again. "You keep telling me that like I'm supposed to believe it. Stop being silly, sweetheart, and make me forget all this."

He pushed her down on the couch, quiet, so as not to wake anyone else, and he kissed her like they were sixteen all over again and nothing else existed.

"Soon, Gillian Wanamaker. Very soon, and then you're all mine," he whispered.

"Stop being silly, sweetheart. I was yours all along."

BROOKE HAD BEEN TO exactly two weddings in her life. Jessica Price's, who had been Dr. Knox's cleaning lady at the chiropractic office, and there was the New Year's Eve in Chicago when she had been paid thirty dollars to be part of the well-wishers at a civil ceremony. Yet, in spite of her less than ideal experiences, Brooke still possessed those girly dreams of huge bouquets of flowers and pink-pearled ribbons and long white dresses. It was completely unsurprising that Gillian had those same girly dreams, as well.

The morning of Gillian and Austen's wedding, the chapel had been transformed into the culmination of Gillian's dreams. The room smelled of lilacs and magic and happily-ever-afters. For one quiet minute, Brooke stood alone in the church, waiting for the magic to seep into her soul. There were always dreams to be found, but now she knew that sometimes dreams lurked in unexpected places. Sometimes magic could be found locked behind black metal gates, hidden among old lumber and engines. Sometimes dreams could be buried behind a black eye-patch and a scarred profile, because those places—the places where hearts feared to tread—hid the most fragile of dreams.

She wrapped her arms around herself, holding those fragile dreams inside her. Gillian would have her magical day, and Brooke was happy for her, and today, of all days, she was going to laugh and sigh and be the perfect wedding guest because this was her family now. This was her life.

Back in the bridal room, Modine Wanamaker was fussing with Gillian's hair, and Mindy had her camera, recording the day for posterity. In the corner stood the flower girl, Carmelita Ruiz's daughter, who was sucking her thumb, eyes large with wonder, because all girls dreamed of huge bouquets of flowers and pink-pearled ribbons.

As for the bride, Gillian looked panicked, and Brooke knew just what to say. "The pianist is already here, all the music is accounted for. The flowers are set up—including the lilacs—the cakes and the food are being put out in the reception hall. The photographer has been here for three hours. Austen and Tyler are in the back, fully dressed, but the groom looks appropriately pale. The preacher isn't here yet, but he had his hospital visits this afternoon, so he's not expected for another half-hour, and you look like a dream."

The panic on Gillian's face disappeared, replaced by the normal resolve. "Wow. I didn't realize how close I was to actually throwing up. This is better. This is good." She flashed Brooke a grateful smile. "You know, I'm glad that Austen had a long-lost sister instead of a long-lost brother, because right now, I need all the support I can get."

Impulsively Brooke hugged her, and then Gillian whispered in her ear. "Someday we'll do this for you, little sister. Just you wait."

JASON PLANTED HIMSELF in a secluded corner outside the church, pacing back and forth, watching the people enter through the wooden doors, people who had no strong fears of entering a church or dressing in a suit or mingling among the masses. Max would be laughing at him now, telling him that a soldier feared nothing. Since Max had feared nothing and gotten blown up in the process, it probably wasn't the best advice.

However, Brooke Hart was inside that church, and if Jason wanted her, if he wanted a real life, it was time to give up the fears, and hopefully not get blown up in the process.

He could hear the ghost of Max's laughter, he could see the familiar face of his father, and Jason looked up to the blue, blue sky, felt the warmth of the sun on his skin and then put a hand on the door, wincing at the loud, creaking sound.

Bring the heat, bring the stupid. It was the Army way.

BROOKE KNEW THE SECOND he walked in the church. From her spot in the second pew, she couldn't see him, but she heard the creak of the door. All eyes were on the bride and groom, who were exchanging their vows.

All eyes except for one. Her skin tingled with awareness, and the air crackled with the magic that had been missing before. Brooke's mouth curved into a contented smile because in a world of love songs and poetic vows, Brooke believed that it was the smallest steps that meant the most.

THE RECEPTION HALL was filled with people dancing, along the walls buffet tables were laden with food and Brooke waited patiently for the Captain to appear.

It didn't take long. He presented himself in front of her, handsome in a black suit which made his eye patch and scar seem dashing.

"May I have this dance?" he asked, waiting until she nodded, before sweeping her into his arms. A smaltzy love song played over the speakers, but Brooke thought it was perfect.

"I like your suit. Is it new?"

"I bought it for you." Such simple words, but the look in his gaze was anything but. She told herself not to get carried away though his words and the dance were all too much, so she burrowed her head on his shoulder, admitting it was a lot nicer than his pillow, which she'd accidentally stolen.

"It was a lovely ceremony. I cried at the end." She unburrowed her head, and looked up at him. "Why didn't you tell me the lawyer called? Mr. Hadley said he spoke to you."

The Captain murmured something uncomplimentary about Mr. Hadley. "I didn't want you to leave. I knew you would, but I didn't want it."

"I would have stayed if you had asked."

"I know, but it wouldn't have been right. You depended on me too much, and I wasn't comfortable with that."

"I will always depend on you. I'm sorry."

"I love you."

"I know." She looked around, and noticed the attention they were getting. For once she didn't mind. "They're staring."

"It's a good thing I'm half blind," he told her, his mouth in a nervous smile, then turning down in a frown. "Brooke, they're staring because I'm the Boo Radley of this town. All my own doing, I fully admit that, but you can't do this. I'm the guy who scavenges the junkyards and the scrap yard, picking up the things that everyone threw out."

She reached up to sooth the frown, and made a silent vow to make him happy because he deserved to be happy. Every day he thought nothing of all the things that he did, all the people that he helped, but in this, Brooke knew that the world depended on the Captain, just as she did.

"I spent my life living in the trash, but you were the first person who ever pulled me out and dusted me off and treated me with respect. I never understood how important that is. Loving me for me. It's not something I'm ever going to forget, and it's why I love you, and why I will always love you. No one else in the world can ever do that for me."

Right then, the song changed and Celine Dion came on, and the dancing slowed and Brooke locked her arms around his neck and kissed him. It was a long and forever kind of kiss, a floating-on-the-ice kiss, and she knew that everyone was staring and she didn't care.

Finally, at long last, Brooke Hart was home.

Epilogue

IT WAS BROOKE'S first Thanksgiving with her family. Gillian and her mother had been baking for three solid days, and there was enough food to feed the masses, but even with all that, Thanksgiving morning had Gillian going on about the giblets, making everyone nervous in the process.

Edie and Tyler had flown down, and Edie was debating with Gillian's mother about the proper way to mash potatoes. Brooke offered to help, but in the end, it was easier to stand alongside the counter and watch everyone yell and argue with a dreamy look on her face. This.

This.

Jason came to stand next to her, a Washington Redskins cap in his hand. "You look like it's Christmas in November."

"It's great, isn't it?"

"It is."

She reached up and touched his scar, then his mouth, watching the warm gray gaze grow hot. She felt the heat slide down her spine, contentment settling firmly in her heart.

"What are my brothers doing?" She used the words a lot.

My brother this. My brother that, and Jason never laughed at her, which she appreciated.

"Don't make me break a promise," he warned.

At that point, Gillian looked up from her stirring, spied Jason, and flashed him an angelic smile. "Jason, darling, can you go find Austen and drag him in here? There's some placemats in the buffet with needlepoint turkeys, and I've got my hands full with the giblets right now."

Brooke smirked. "You're going to have to break that promise."

ALARMED, JASON LOOKED at his one true love and mouthed, "Needlepoint turkeys?" But she only smiled.

Sadly realizing he had no choice in the matter, Jason approached the living room, which he had privately termed the DMZ. Austen and Tyler were gone, as was Emmett Wanamaker, and at that point, Jason considered his task complete. But then he sighed because Brooke had high expectations for this family dinner, and while he thought turkey placemats were slightly demeaning, he knew that Brooke was loving it all, and it made all the hell worth it.

Almost all the hell worth it.

Hell, yeah, it was worth it.

He found them outside, four folding chairs huddled around a tiny black and white TV, watching football. Cowboys and Redskins.

Now that was Thanksgiving.

"Who's winning?" Jason asked, watching as the Cowboy quarterback threw an interception right into the arms of the Skins receiver.

"Skins up by seven," Austen answered.

Jason shrugged innocently. "Don't blame me because your boys are playing like girls."

Emmett Wanamaker glared, but Jason glared back, and

frankly, very few people could outglare a one-eyed man. Naturally, Emmett caved. "Gillian wants you to find placemats," he told Austen, doing what he'd promised. "They're in the buffet. Somewhere."

Austen looked at his father-in-law for help. "What placemats?"

Emmett's eyes were fixed on the screen, watching as the Redskins lined up on the Cowboys' seven. "Damned needlepoint turkeys. They're going to be accidentally destroyed in a fire someday, mark my words."

"Talk to Austen then," Tyler said with a laugh. "He's great at accidentally setting fires."

Austen shoved his brother in the ribs, and then the Redskins scored and Jason let out an all-American hoo-yah. He could just imagine his own family celebrating the same moment.

It was twenty minutes later when Brooke found him there, having pulled up another chair, as she leaned over his back she pressed a small kiss against his ear.

"Happy Thanksgiving," she whispered.

Jason smiled at her, counting her freckles, counting his blessings, and decided that this family thing was a fine thing after all.

* * * * *

COMING NEXT MONTH

Available September 27, 2011

You can find more information on upcoming
Harlequin® titles, free excerpts and more at
www.HarlequinInsideRomance.com.

HBCNM0911

REQUEST YOUR FREE BOOKS!
2 FREE NOVELS PLUS 2 FREE GIFTS!

red-hot reads!

*Harlequin Romantic Suspense presents the latest book
in the scorching new* KELLEY LEGACY *miniseries
from best-loved veteran series author Carla Cassidy*

*Scandal is the name of the game as the Kelley family fights
to preserve their legacy, their hearts...and their lives.*

*Read on for an excerpt from the fourth title
RANCHER UNDER COVER*

*Available October 2011
from Harlequin Romantic Suspense*

"**W**ould you like a drink?" Caitlin asked as she walked
to the minibar in the corner of the room. She felt as if she
needed to chug a beer or two for courage.

"No, thanks. I'm not much of a drinking man," he
replied.

She raised an eyebrow and looked at him curiously as she
poured herself a glass of wine. "A ranch hand who doesn't
enjoy a drink? I think maybe that's a first."

He smiled easily. "There was a six-month period in my
life when I drank too much. I pulled myself out of the bottom of a bottle a little over seven years ago and I've never
looked back."

"That's admirable, to know you have a problem and then
fix it."

Those broad shoulders of his moved up and down in
an easy shrug. "I don't know how admirable it was, all I
knew at the time was that I had a choice to make between
living and dying and I decided living was definitely more
appealing."

She wanted to ask him what had happened preceding
that six-month period that had plunged him into the bottom

of the bottle, but she didn't want to know too much about him. Personal information might produce a false sense of intimacy that she didn't need, didn't want in her life.

"Please, sit down," she said, and gestured him to the table. She had never felt so on edge, so awkward in her life.

"After you," he replied.

She was aware of his gaze intensely focused on her as she rounded the table and sat in the chair, and she wanted to tell him to stop looking at her as if she were a delectable dessert he intended to savor later.

Watch Caitlin and Rhett's sensual saga unfold amidst the shocking, ripped-from-the-headlines drama of the Kelley Legacy miniseries in

RANCHER UNDER COVER

Available October 2011 only from Harlequin Romantic Suspense, wherever books are sold.

USA TODAY bestselling author

Carol Marinelli

brings you her new romance

HEART OF THE DESERT

One searing kiss is all it takes for Georgie to know
Sheikh Prince Ibrahim is trouble....

But, trapped in the swirling sands, Georgie finally
surrenders to the brooding rebel prince—yet the
law of his land decrees that she can never
really be his....

Available October 2011.

Available only from Harlequin Presents®.

www.Harlequin.com

HP13020